Giant Frog, Methane Smog, and Super Speed to Ganymede

ROBERT K. LEET

ISBN 978-1-7345189-3-1

Published by
Fringe Tree Press
Port Washington, New York

Cover and interior design by Maria Socolof

Chapter 1

Beulah, North Dakota: It was Sunday, December 16, 2035. Ramon Stavite stepped out of his house at about 8 a.m. to see how much snow had accumulated overnight. "Only six or seven inches," he mumbled to himself as he gazed toward the grove of trees at the edge of his property.

He noticed some large tracks and went down the slope to check them out. "Mother of Mephistopheles! What the devil is this?" he exclaimed when he spotted the strange footprints. "Looks like a two-legged being. And the size and shape of these prints are amazing! Whoever or whatever this thing was must have been mighty tall to have such a long stride. They look like they're from huge webbed feet with five toes. And there's a smaller five-digit print, too. Maybe this 'thing' lost its balance and put out an arm to steady himself after slipping on some ice."

"Maybe a long-legged ostrich escaped from some zoo?" suggested his twelve-year old son, who had come down to join his father.

"I think ostriches only have a couple of toes, and I don't know a thing about their arms or hands," Ramon replied. His son, Edwardo, wanted to follow the tracks, but his mother's freshly made pancakes dissuaded him.

The next day, Ramon drove to the Great Plains Synfuels Plant (a subsidiary of the Dakota Gasification Co.) in Beulah where he worked. Through the complex process of gasification of lignite coal, his company produced synthetic natural gas (SNG), which is comprised of about ninety percent methane. They also liquefied the SNG at -260°F and stored it in cryogenic tanks. This liquefied natural gas (LNG) was used much less frequently than the gaseous form, but this condensed liquid, stored in these ultra-cold tanks, was much easier to transport.

When Ramon arrived at work, he learned there had been a break-in at the large refrigerated shed that housed the storage containers of LNG. In addition to storing a few massive cryogenic tanks, the frigid hut had a holding area with several smaller, easily handled vessels, each weighing seventy-five pounds. The heavy door to the hut had been torn open and two of the smaller LNG containers were missing. Had someone (or something) known what was being produced and stored in this facility?

Breaking into the cold house was no small feat due to the thick, insulated, heavy, metal shed door. It was also "no small *feet*" that had left their tracks in the snow outside the shed. Large pad-like footprints perfectly matched those that Ramon had seen on his property.

"Those tracks are kind of weird" was the consensus of the work crew at the Gasification complex.

Ramon chipped in: "Those are the same tracks that went past my house—some five miles away. Whoever it was made it onto some of the main roads that were free of snow, so I didn't get a good look as to where it was heading."

"Maybe it's some clown wearing funny feet," someone suggested.

"Maybe," Ramon replied, "but he must have been mighty strong to break in and haul away a couple of seventy-five-pound methane containers."

The morning foreman said he would report the incident to the police, and since no more damage had occurred, they all went back to work. The police weren't able to get any further in finding the culprit. The weird tracks seemed to stop altogether after the perpetrator reached the highway.

The USA at this time was in a bit of turmoil. Years earlier, there had been many attacks by the radical ISIS/ISIL forces on New York City, Portland, Oregon, and San Francisco, to name a few. There had also been a slow, smoldering tension with North Korea that started back with their leader Kim Jong-un(hinged). North Korea continued to shower their missile "tests" over the heads of South Koreans and around the East China Sea and the Sea of Japan—close enough to make the Japanese very jittery. Just to make things a little worse, the American president, Donald Trump, antagonized, aggravated, and insulted so many nations, both friend and foe, that the American citizens were on edge. Fearing an attack from somewhere, they began chanting, "Donald—Duck!" It didn't take very long before Trump was declared *non compos mentis* and removed from office by a "fake" judge and an "insane" psychiatric consortium.

Before the world's gas and oil supplies were augmented by findings of large underground natural gas and oil fields under Texas, Middle America, and the Mediterranean Sea, there was a burgeoning of some industrial plants (such as the Dakota Gasification Co.) to continue using lignite coal to make SNG. Two of the first such companies were in Bismarck and Beulah, North Dakota.

Not only did there seem to be a worsening of relationships among countries, but the condition of the Earth itself seemed to be worsening—ballooning world population; shortages of water, oil, food, medicines; and the haunting global warming. It was a question not only of whether the USA would survive, but if Planet Earth itself was headed in a downward spiral. Throughout the 4.6 billion years since the Earth had formed, there were five (or more?) major extinctions. Would this be the beginning of the sixth extinction—as was so well presented by Elizabeth Kolbert in her 2014 book *The Sixth Extinction*?

Temperatures were increasing, glaciers and icebergs were melting. Many ocean-dwelling organisms were having trouble adapting. Even the polar bears were being disrupted by the overheated atmosphere and the loss of their frozen habitat.

Did these atmospheric changes have anything to do with the strange break-in at Beulah, ND, and the absconding with the two portable methane tanks? Far (very far!) from it. There wasn't an atmospheric tie-in with the break-in, but there was a solar system connection.

When the solar system's planets were formed some 4.6 billion years ago, the giant gas planet Jupiter formed in relatively close proximity to another gas giant planet (at least this is what many astronomers have theorized—but it was possible that it could also have been a "rocky" planet more like

Earth). Jupiter's orbital path in those early centuries was erratic and at one point Jupiter, it has been theorized, crossed a little too close to this other slightly smaller planet, and a "gravitational slingshot" occurred. This sent the smaller planet far away to the outer regions of the Kuiper belt—beyond Saturn, Uranus, and Neptune. This was so far out that no telescopes could visualize it. Only the effect upon the surrounding asteroids' orbital trajectories made it very likely there was a relatively large body that was creating this disturbance. Even without being able to see this large body, astronomers and astrophysicists were surmising this was Planet Nine ("IXon"). Pluto had previously been number nine until it was reclassified as a dwarf planet and could no longer play with the big boys.

So, if this new Planet IXon was part of the solar system, how did it differ from any of the other planets? When both Planet IXon and Planet Earth first began, they had hot environments of mostly carbon dioxide (CO_2) and methane. Over a billion years or so, Earth developed a new bacterial strain—cyanobacteria. Still found in some Australian formations (and known as stromatolites), the cyanobacteria consumed CO_2 as an energy source and gave off a gas that would eventually dominate the Earth's atmosphere—oxygen.

An oxygen-saturated condition leads to a cooling atmosphere. This cooling of Planet Earth, over eons, led to a massive ice age (called Snowball Earth), which eliminated almost all living organisms, except for a few microbes. This was the first great extinction. This Snowball Earth would continue off and on interspersed with melting and heating from heavy, prolonged volcanic activity around the globe and possibly from changes in the Sun's energy output or the tilting of the Earth's axis.

It took the Earth until about three million years ago to achieve a sustainable atmosphere, allowing human ancestors to come down from the trees and began their bipedal journey from *Australopithecus africanus* to *Homo sapiens* (*H. sapiens* arrived approximately 130,000 years ago). (Lucy was one of the first australopithecines discovered. The archeologist who uncovered her skeletal remains and who named her, happened to be an aficionado of Beatles music—especially their *Lucy in the Sky with Diamonds*.)

The wayward orphan, Planet IXon, ostracized by Jupiter (by Jove!), continued on with its CO_2- and methane-dominated atmosphere. This type of gaseous atmosphere creates a global warming effect. IXon also had significant internal warming from volcanic activity, but never had any cyanobacteria to provide oxygen. In the super-cold reaches of the outer Kuiper belt, IXon began developing its own form of life. There were many large underground caverns on IXon, warmed by deep underground calderas of molten lava, not dissimilar to calderas like the one under Yellowstone National Park in Wyoming that heats the Old Faithful geyser.

As noted, cyanobacteria on Earth produced an oxygen atmosphere a billion or more (Earth) years ago. On IXon, the caldera (volcanic) warming allowed for the development of methane-producing bacteria, which then created a methane-dominant atmosphere. The exact mechanism that allowed this flourishing was not known.

Methane gas was prevalent in the atmosphere and in the swampy subterranean lakes and rivers of IXon. As fauna and flora evolved, was there something special in the murky underground water (other than the marsh gases, methane, etc.)? Whatever was in these pools had a dramatic effect on rapid-growing frogs, salamanders, snakes, and other amphibians and reptiles. There were no dinosaurs on IXon, but some of the now larger-than-average frogs were reminiscent of the plant-eating sauropods on Earth. The frogs not only grew in size, but over another million-plus years, their expanded heads developed a respectable brain and mind intelligence. This increased intellect was even greater in the one and only giant Ranasaurus (as it would be named later by Earthlings after years of puzzling about this giant alien—more about that later).

The rapid evolution that occurred on IXon showed some spectacular outcomes. The exceptionally large Ranasaurus had developed into a real terror. This frog was a genetic anomaly that had developed legs that were about four times larger and ten times stronger than any of the rest of the frogs in the pond.

One of the other notable features of Ranasaurus, and the smaller species of frogs, was the development of enlarged, sophisticated, super spiracles along the lateral abdomen similar to the grasshopper's spiracles on Earth. The IXonian spiracles had a dual passageway that could separate gaseous and liquid methane and maintain a circulatory and respiratory function without requiring separate lungs and heart.

The Super Anomalous Ranasaurus was the only one that had developed arms and prehensile hands. Most of the other frog species had short "alligator arms" that could scoop and cradle, but had no grasping ability like big Rana, much to the dismay of his littler brethren. All of the frog species appeared to have belligerent personae and at a time when IXon had a period of reduced volcanic activity and the vegetation throughout the cavernous underworld became diminished with the ensuing colder period, the Swamp Wars took place.

The frogs dominated over other amphibians, snakes, poisonous herbivores, and even the larger number of non-poisonous, passive swamp dwellers (one might call them *marsh mellows*). But with food shortages still present, the frogs began dwindling—the prehensile, two-fisted frog was one of the few Rana (frog) species that survived. This one over-powering frog, who stood out among all the others, was Ranasaurus the Large. If they had played baseball on IXon, this would be Babe Ruth, Mickey Mantle, and Aaron Judge all rolled into one. Babe-Mick-Aaron Frog could run faster, jump higher, and hit harder than any other frog in the swamp. When it came to sending an envoy to any strange, unknown place, this would be the *Ranaway* #1 choice.

In addition to the evolving Ranasaurus, IXon had an unrecognizable (to Earthlings) creature with gnome-like features—small arms and legs, and a brain that had been able, over the millions of years, to far outperform the best and fastest computers on Earth, exceeding both petaFLOPS and exaFLOPS computer speed.

Even with a better-than-average intelligence, Ranasaurus had nowhere near the intellectual ability of the supercomputerized brains of these IXonian creatures (from some breakaway evolutionary species?). They had quite rapidly evolved and developed superior skills in producing robots that could survive for thousands of years (in Earth time). These robots became the ruling class of this planet that was ten times larger than Earth. A group of small, brainy robotic scientists constituted the leaders and rulers of this strange planet. They lived apart from the rest of the inhabitants of IXon (probably in what was called—*gnome mansland?*).

Chapter 2

I Xonians had some difficulties similar to those of the Earthlings. On Earth there were problems with diminishing supplies of water, gas, oil, and food for an ever-enlarging population (eight billion plus). In addition, there was persistent global warming. The IXonians did not have a population explosion as large as Earth's, but there was a definite decrease in methane production. Their centuries-long decrease in volcanic warming was compromising the planet's ability to maintain flourishing bacterial colonies that were producing the life-sustaining methane.

IXon had advanced their spacecraft (all robotically operated) to the point where they surpassed what the Earth's scientists had done. They perfected nuclear pulse propulsion, fusion-powered rockets, and laser-propelled, huge lightweight sails. So far though, they hadn't come up with any antimatter-based propulsion, but they created several dozen scout airships (rocket-planes), which they felt could search out other sources of methane gases, liquids, and solids. The small, brainy, robotic, non-methane-dependent IXon scientists developed a process somewhat similar to the Earth's Sabatier method used to produce methane:

$$CO_2 + 4H_2 \rightarrow CH_4 \text{ (methane)} + 2H_2O.$$

However, this method didn't produce sufficient quantities of methane to provide power for the machines and heating—especially on the surface of the planet where they had some methane-heated observation laboratories and telescopic facilities. They also needed large quantities of methane to power their rockets and exploratory aircraft.

Their original searches for methane were carried out on and around the gas giants Saturn, Neptune, and Uranus. Especially interesting were the surface lakes of methane found on Saturn's moon Titan. Also, Enceladus, another one of Saturn's moons, had plumes of small amounts of methane emanating from subsurface oceans of water. IXon had six moons, but none appeared to have sufficient methane to sustain the mother planet. There was some interest in Neptune's moon Triton (not Titan), which is the only moon in the solar system to have a retrograde orbit (goes in the opposite direction from the orbits of the other moons). There had been some methane in the region of Triton, but there seemed to be more plumes of water than methane, so the IXonians concentrated their efforts on Saturn's moons Titan and Enceladus, even though the initial samples of methane they brought back from the lakes of Titan had some impurities.

The IXonians had a number of medium- and long-range rocket-planes, which they manned with robotic pilots and crews. Their initial forays throughout the Kuiper belt did not turn up any caches of their precious CH_4. When they ventured farther and came across Saturn's largest moon, Titan, where they found large lakes of hydrocarbons (methane, propane, ethane, etc.), there were signs that someone else had already visited Titan.

Back in 2004, after a seven-year trip from Earth to Titan, the Cassini-Huygens mission (a joint endeavor of USA's NASA, the European Space Agency, and the Italian Space Agency) had dropped the Huygens probe down on the surface of Titan. There were only a few brief minutes that the Huygens could transmit information up to the Cassini spacecraft. After Cassini moved out of range, the Huygens probe was left on Titan while the Cassini orbiter went on to study Saturn and environs before being intentionally destroyed in September 2017 when its energy source was exhausted.

There were some very strong winds on Titan's surface. A lot of surface dirt and moisture partially covered the now incommunicative Huygens probe. It was buffeted about, but not completely covered up or destroyed. The strange markings on the probe were a puzzle, but the dwarf-like brainiacs on IXon had a suspicion that it was most likely from one of the inner planets closer to the Sun—the *rocky* planets, as opposed to the *gas* outer planets of Jupiter, Saturn, Uranus, and Neptune.

In all of the research into space that the IXonians had done, they were fascinated by the barely visible Blue Planet, which they suspected had an important water supply. The blue color, they figured, was from large amounts of surface water— oceans? The consensus of the astrophysicists was that it would be very interesting to find out more about this Blue Planet. They decided they needed to get closer to the inner planets because of the vast distances that separated IXon from the rest of the solar system. With the superfast rocket-planes that IXon had, they felt that getting to one of Jupiter's moons would bring them close enough to Planet Blue to investigate it, and hopefully far enough away to escape if any dangerous situations arose. With all the research that the IXonian scientists had done, they figured that this aberrant-looking planet might have been the one that sent some sort of device to land on Titan. The real unknown was what sort of propulsion could have been used, and how long a trip could it have been? IXon was used to dealing with more advanced propulsion systems (compared to Earth's), and they had no way of knowing how long a flight from Earth to Titan might have taken. They decided to set up an advanced, distant base on Jupiter's largest moon, Ganymede, which didn't appear to have all the volcanic activity that Io (Jupiter's innermost moon) had.

The interest in investigating this strange Blue Planet was not just curiosity. The samples of the hydrocarbons from Titan—methane, ethane, etc.—that they had obtained from the Kraken Mare (the largest known body of liquid on the surface of Titan) and Ladoga Lacus [named by Americans for the Russian Lake Ladoga that had provided a route for supplies to Leningrad (now St. Petersburg) during WWII], contained a lot of impurities compared to the methane on IXon, and the IXonians hoped that the Blue Planet might have a purer form of methane.

They had already set up a telescope base on a different moon of Saturn (Mimas) to get a closer look at the solar system environs. The views they got of Jupiter and its moons were quite good, but there still was not a very distinct vision of Mars, Earth, or Venus. Mercury remained just a small blur.

In the group meeting of the IXon leaders, the written language of plans and past histories was a conglomeration of zeros, ones, and pictograms (not unlike Egyptian hieroglyphs), and their verbal communication was in varying levels of metallic sounds and cadences—quite understandable to most of those present. If they didn't agree with a statement, they probably uttered something like "IXnay!"

The upshot of the meeting was that they would need some aquatic creature to do much of the exploring on the Blue Planet because they were anticipating a watery environment. Of all the mechanical robots that were available, there were none that could do any swimming or jumping that might be required in an unknown new environment with apparent oceans. Their ideal candidate for this mission would be the one and only giant frog—the supersized Ranasaurus. It was certainly the number one candidate. However, they needed the Ranasaurus to have a more sophisticated communication system so that it could quickly analyze and adapt to rapidly changing events and be able to coordinate with the scout rocket-planes and the IXon outpost on Ganymede. To achieve this, they needed a very intricate transplantation of a supercomputerized brain-communicator onto the upper body and neck of the Rana. They would also need to attach fine fiber-metallic wires to the body and legs of the frog, which would be controlled by both the visual and sensory input to the new brain, and would also have return signals relayed from the brain to the body to ensure an almost instant reaction and an immediate ability to get out of harms way or proceed in a different direction. This would create an android Ranatron (Frogdroid)—the likes of which the solar system had never seen.

Although the sensory inputs and muscle responses were pretty well coordinated, there still was concern for the maintenance of the non-mechanical parts of the Frogdroid, which required liquid or gaseous forms of methane to nourish the powerful legs, the less powerful arms, and the prehensile webbed "hands." While the brainiac IXonians had taken many long days (approximately 300 Earth days) to ready the Ranatron physically, another problem was how to keep an adequate supply of methane available to the 'Tron when he was far afield on some distant planet. There would have to be some serious rationing of the methane usage on Planet IXon, and a decent amount of methane for the scout rocket-planes to have some reserve for the Big Frog if needed. Since there had been no way of being certain what they would find on the Blue Planet in terms of methane, the IXonians began sending their superfast scout rockets from Ganymede with advanced chromatographic equipment that could test some of the components of the Blue Planet's atmosphere. It was at this time that there began to be many reports on Earth of "flying saucers."

There had been many such reports starting back in the late 1940s with the Roswell, New Mexico hullabaloo that didn't prove to be anything alien, but kept the UFO suspicions going on for decades. These claims of possible alien invaders finally began to subside, until the IXon scout planes arrived close to Earth in their search of any available methane.

The IXon plan was to have the one large, strong Randroid as the primary explorer, and have several of the all-robotic scout planes view the Blue Planet from above and record as best they could the topography, sample the atmosphere, and view any other objects within range of their somewhat limited telecameras.

There were six robotically controlled scout rockets that made the very lengthy trip from IXon to Ganymede—followed by more scouts and methane tanker planes carrying heavy, reinforced-metal cryogenic tanks of methane. There did not appear to be any appreciable methane in Jupiter's largest moons: Io, Europa, Callisto, and Ganymede. However, there was considerable water on several of the moons—including the copious salt water beneath the ice on Ganymede. The subsurface water on Europa was believed to be kept liquid by the tidal pull (also known as tidal flexing) associated with the giant Jupiter, which would agitate the water, and thus prevent freezing.

The IXon scout planes had super-powered nuclear pulse propulsion with additional jet power to enable them to make quick feints and fast getaways once they entered the Earth's atmosphere, in case they needed escapes or rapid changes in direction. The IXon scientists, operating out of their lab on Ganymede, got a good spectroscopic analysis of Earth's atmosphere and realized there would be no easy access to methane unless it might be at the site of some suboceanic region as had been present in the Pacific Ocean. The scouts also identified methane vapors emanating from some swampy regions and over the Black Sea north of Turkey.

In the United States and around the world, fracking (hydraulic fracturing) began in 1947. As of 2012, two-and-a-half-million fracking jobs had been created worldwide—over one-third of those were in the USA. These fracking sites produced flows of shale oil and shale gas (also called "tight" oil and gas). The fracking posed potential environmental impacts, including risk of ground and surface water contamination and risks of triggering earthquakes. Proppant (grains of sand, ceramic, or other particulate matter) was used to keep the fractures from closing. Methanol [methyl alcohol (CH_3-OH)] was used as a corrosion inhibitor during fracking (and methane could be obtained from methanol by a heating process called gasification). Since this was a source of methane that could leak into the atmosphere, it encouraged the IXonians to do some more close-up researching.

How much methane could be produced on the Blue Planet? Some estimates came from biochemists, chemical engineers, and geologists who had studied the largest extinction on Earth. This extinction was called the "Great Dying," which occurred about 250 million years ago. There have been a number of hypotheses as to the cause(s) of this extinction, which wiped out about ninety-five percent of all the species on Earth.

One of the theories was that there were thousands of years of active volcanoes that pumped carbon dioxide, methane, and sulphurous gases into the atmosphere. Another leading theory, by Gregory Ryskin, a biochemical engineer from Northwestern University, was that the major cause was due to the worldwide methane explosions from deep seabeds of methane hydrates.

With the rising temperatures from all the volcanic activity, the frozen methyl hydrate (clathrate) beds that lined the shores (littoral regions) melted and released tons of methane into the atmosphere. This was responsible for a choking, fiery conflagration (the volatile methane is easily flammable especially when ignited by lightening), overheating the atmosphere, and slowly eradicating the vast number of Earth's species.

Chapter 3

We last left the Ranatron (Ranasaurus, Randroid, Ranegade, *Frogissimus giganticus*)—as he would be called by various observers on Earth—traipsing through the snow in North Dakota after heisting two containers of liquid methane from the Great Plains Synfuels Plant in Beulah, North Dakota on December 16, 2035. The refueling of the lower body of the Ranatron had to take place every two to three months depending on how vigorous his activity was. Liquid or gaseous methane could be introduced into the spiracle network of this alien frog and shunted to the various muscles. The mechanical structure of the upper chest of Rana contained a fibro-elastic pump. The methane refueled through the spiracles would be sent to the chest pump and then directed to the areas that needed more strength or power. The capacity of the pump could usually last for two to three months of moderate muscular activity.

The Ranatron hadn't been seen by any Earthlings before his visit to Beulah. He descended through the Earth's atmosphere at a very slow pace thanks to the efficient retrofiring that prevented his scout vehicle from overheating. The IXon scientists who analyzed the chemical make-up and concentration of the Earth's atmosphere figured a parachute, in addition to the retro-rocket, would give the scout vehicle the chance of a safe landing. However, the vehicle wasn't able to avoid the eastern red cedar, juniper, and pine trees in a grove in the North Dakota hills. Rana wasn't damaged, but his rocket-plane was, and its robotic pilot looked like it was ready for the scrap heap or made into a Mixmaster.

There were a number of uninhabited caves around Beulah, ND. Rana was near one that rivaled the large Bear Cave in the southwest part of North Dakota. His scout ship had accessory superstrength carbon wheels and was small enough for Rana to drag the damaged ship into the depths of the cave where he covered it with branches. The high winds that swept over this area quickly covered both the crash site and Rana's big footprints with snow and brush.

Although the footprints leading away from the cave were obscured, the tracks outside the Dakota Gasification Company were still fresh and visible. Ramon Stavite, the first to spot these strange large footprints, stirred up a lot of interest and curiosity among his co-workers. The bosses in the company were also concerned about the stolen liquid methane tanks.

"Do you think this phenomenon is somehow related to Bigfoot/Yeti/Sasquatch/Abominable Snowman?" was voiced by most of the workers.

Bigfoot was the name given to large (ape-like?—frog-like?) footprints in the snow in Del Norte County in Northern California. Gerald Crew, a native of Buff Creek in Del Norte County, made the footprint casts. These prints were ostensibly similar (or the same as) the descriptions of Sasquatch footprints.

<u>Sasquatch</u> was alleged to be a primate/person hybrid. The name came from the native dialect of residents of Fraser Valley in the Pacific Northwest and parts of Vancouver Island, British Columbia, Canada.

<u>The Yeti</u> was supposed to have frequented areas around the Himalayan mountains in South Central Asia (including Mt. Everest). Some indigenous people of the Himalayas worshiped this large ape-man and gave him (it?) the name Yeti—"The Glacial Being."

<u>The Abominable Snowman</u> was named by a native, also from the Mt. Everest region, who called this creature "*Metoh-Kangmi*" (man-bear-snowman) which became anglicized to Abominable Snowman.

Pictures taken by the North Dakotans were analyzed carefully by many specialists—all of whom seemed to agree these were giant-sized frog prints, but the couple of imprints in the snow where the Ranatron had slipped or stumbled did not show any of the characteristics of normal, earthly frog forelegs. This was because the giant Ranatron had some intricate surgery to improve his prehensile hands with a combination of muscle and mechanical wiring (*handroid* surgery?).

While the Earth's scientists were trying to solve the mystery of this "New Bigfoot" or as some old-timers suggested, harking back to a slightly altered 1940s song *Flat Foot 'Froggie' with the Floy Floy* (apologies to Slim Gaillard, Count Basie, *et al.*), the workers from the Gasification Company in Beulah, ND were more intent on trying to follow the trail of this strange "thing."

"I don't recall anything like big frog feet being associated with all the Bigfoot sightings in the Northwest USA and

Canada," Ramon Stavite said to the little group that had decided to follow the "creature."

"And it doesn't sound like the Abominable Snowman or any of the other mysterious creatures . . . at least . . . not Yeti," Buddy "Cornball" Oleander replied, while somebody heaved a snowball at him.

Ranatron went north toward Lake Sakakawea (the Americans preferred the spelling Sacajawea—after the Shoshone woman who aided and interpreted for Lewis and Clark on their expedition to the Pacific coast). The wind and swirling snow followed the Ranatron as it traveled north in a wandering way. The compass that had been installed in Rana's computer head would be helpful in finding his direction since the magnetic poles in both Earth and IXon were oriented toward a similar positioning. He would also be guided by the scout planes, which could direct him toward regions where there was chromatographic evidence of increased methane in the atmosphere.

As Rana plodded north, he reached the town of New Salem, ND and came face to face with Salem Sue, a thirty-eight-foot-high and fifty-foot-long fiberglass cow. How was this gigantocow interpreted by the analysts on Ganymede and back on IXon when they received transmissions of this motionless, obviously inanimate, statue? The IXonians' concern was whether this *moo-umental* beast actually represented a species of mega-moos on Earth that could be a threat to Rana. Rana did feel a little jumpy (after all he was a frog) at the sight of the statue—but he wasn't truly cowed. It would be quite a while before he would see any real live bovine creatures. Rana was probably fortunate that he hadn't wandered east toward Jamestown, ND where there was an equally *hu-moo-ngus* statue of a big, bouncy Bison bull—just a bit bigger and more imposing than sweet Salem Sue.

With his captured containers of liquid methane, Rana could go at least several more weeks with the liquid that could convert to the gaseous form of methane. The frigid liquid was warmed to its gaseous phase by heating devices planted internally in Rana's chest and lower abdomen; his internal thermostat moderated the temperature. The device in his chest allowed the gas to more easily traverse the smaller arteries in the arms and upper torso. The one in his lower abdomen helped warm his legs, as did the churning action of his powerful leg muscles.

The supercomputer brain was capable of operating (with its rust-proof parts) for many months without any repair or rejuvenation. The message that had been programmed into the Rana brain was to seek out any and all sources of methane and indicate how difficult it would be to get it into a usable form for transport or immediate use as the conditions required or allowed.

The spectrographic instruments that the IXonians were using were not penetrating enough to pick up any of the very deep subsurface locations of the Earth's methane sources. An exception to this seemed to be along the shorelines, for example, in Alaska, the Arctic, and Turkey. The icy methane clathrates in these areas were just slightly submerged, some down to 300 to 500 meters below water level. With the temperatures rising so rapidly due to global warming, the clathrates in the shallower regions began melting and further exacerbating the overheated atmosphere with methane and CO_2.

Several times in the past 200-plus million years on Earth, when there was substantial global warming, large amounts of methane had eluted from the coastal clathrates. There were also other causes of major methane accumulations. At times, numerous large earthquakes that reached the shorelines would dislodge many of the clathrates. At other times, when the tectonic plates had collided into each other, many deep reservoirs of methane were released into the atmosphere from the ocean beds and also from the permafrost. And as already mentioned, a couple of scientists had the theory that the biggest extinction on Earth (the "Great Dying") was caused by massive amounts of methane liberated into the atmosphere, possibly in conjunction with extreme global warming and prolonged volcanic activity.

While waiting to hear what was happening with the adventures of the Roaming Rana, the IXon strategists were considering the possible reactions that they might expect from the Earth's inhabitants. Would there be a friendly reception, or would the Earthlings look upon Rambling Rana as an alien invader? In the back of the IXonian supercomputer minds was the collective agreement that the scout planes should be armed in case the reception on Earth was more belligerent than benign. Missiles, rapid-fire machine guns, and rocket-launchers were installed in the speedy, shifty methane-jet-aided scouts— with the hope that they wouldn't need them if the Earth dwellers had a soft spot for frogs. If they only knew, they could have dropped Rana off in France.

Before the IXonians had launched their super frog, they spent over a year getting a visual survey of the Earth, looking to ascertain the topography and analyze the atmosphere to try to locate any methane hot spots. They also analyzed the content of the Earth's atmosphere (oxygen, CO_2, nitrogen, etc.) to be sure their scout planes wouldn't have any problems when they flew close to the Earth's surface. They had arranged a relay pattern to have planes return for refueling by tanker planes about half the distance from Earth to Ganymede. The nuclear pulse propulsion allowed the scouts to travel huge distances in much less time than any of Earth's planes, so the refueling was not a big problem. The auxiliary jet engine that had been added to the scout planes provided a quick burst of power for rapid changes of direction to avoid any enemies that might be chasing them. The IXonians on their home planet had experimented with oxygen (derived from electrolysis of H_2O) and created a methane plus liquid oxygen jet engine.

The Ranatron managed to stay out of sight of any humans for the first couple of weeks during the winter when the wind and snow tended to disguise the direction in which he was heading. Judging from the size of the footprints and the distance between each step, indicating a very long stride, the general conclusion among several who had observed the tracks seemed to be that this being was some sort of giant frog. They suspected it might be a very tall impersonator who was trying to advertise some strange product. Others felt a bit more anxious and began revisiting many of the old fearsome Abominable Snowman and Bigfoot stories.

The workers at the Great Plains Synfuels Plant in Beulah were still scratching their heads about why this strange web-footed being would want heavy, portable cryogenic containers of liquid methane.

On one of the repeat fly-overs by the IXon scout planes, the pilots noted an increasing amount of methane gas around the borders of the Arctic Ocean. Was this due to the rapid increase of global warming? To get a clearer picture of the Arctic area, the pilots sent the Ranatron a message consisting of IXonian language squeaks, pauses, dots, dashes, and other sounds, which were totally unintelligible to the Earthlings. The message said he should continue his northerly course up from the Dakotas and through Canada until he could get an up-close assessment of how great a supply of methane there might be.

The stories surrounding the frog-monster began to catch on quickly in the area around the Dakotas and into southern Canada—Manitoba and Saskatchewan. The elusiveness of the web-footed creature had some calling it the Ranaway Roamer.

There were a number of high fences in and around Winnipeg, Manitoba. The Rana had easily hopped over a couple of these without being noticed, but on a third ten-foot-high metal fence, some late night partygoers on the outskirts of Winnipeg spotted him.

In addition to the great strength of the Ranatron's legs and his amazing jumping ability, he was able to swim very long distances underwater. The temperature control signals sent from its supercomputer head to the thermostat in 'Tron's abdomen would keep him warm and functioning even in the extremely cold waters thanks to the methane that could be utilized in either the liquid or gaseous phase. The 'Tron didn't need to breathe, unlike many of the Earth's species (whales, dolphins, seals, sea turtles), so he could travel many miles under Arctic sea ice if necessary.

Not only did the "brain" of the Ranatron have exceptional capabilities for thinking, planning, and acting, it was encased in an air and watertight carbon-plastic hood that would prevent rusting or other destructive forces from causing the "brain" to fail. The hood had clear windows to "see" and receptors to "hear"—albeit some of these visual and auditory recordings were less than perfect.

After the night revelers in Winnipeg had let the police and the local news reporters know of the amazing leaping feats, and the word had been passed on to the scientific community around the world, the intrigue became even greater. The scientific people had no easy way to figure out how this huge demi-frog could perform such incredible feats—running (loping was more like it), jumping, swimming, etc.—unless some sort of transmission controlled some mechanical or elastic components. But where had this strange being come from? Had some of the Jihadists from the scientific centers in the Middle East come up with a way to frighten the masses and have them, at least for a little while, focus on something other than the attempts of ISIS to take over the world?

American roboticists had developed a small jumping robot called Salto (from the Latin *saltare*: to jump), but this robot was about a foot or less in height, weighing about two pounds. This masterpiece of robotics could jump a magnificent twenty-two inches off the ground—not quite in Rana's class.

While the scientific crowd was scratching its collective head, the people in the North and West were all discussing and puzzling over this really, really Big Foot—and whether this Big (Frog) Foot was in some way a real danger. The comic book crowd seemed to feel this was some manifestation of Superman—faster than a speeding bullet, more powerful than a locomotive, able to leap tall buildings in a single bound! "Look! On the ground, or up in the air! It's a bird? . . . It's a plane? . . . It's Super Frog!" There were also a few "Holy amphibians, Batman! What evil web (foot?) are you weaving?"

Well, our rapid Ranatron wasn't concerned about what people were thinking—he was on a mission to locate methane supplies wherever he could. The first destination that the IXonian "Niner" miners had in mind was to investigate the littoral zone of the ocean, which had the greatest possibility of releasing methane due to the increasing heat from global warming. Their second destination was the tundra where some methane gas also could have escaped due to permafrost melting, also a result of global warming. The methane could be collected by some follow-up missions with special equipment and frozen into liquid form—which made transport in large amounts so much easier.

The methane in the atmosphere was an even more potent agent than CO_2 in contributing to global warming. "How long will it take before the whole planet succumbs to this heat?" the meteorologists, farmers, fishermen, and basically the whole world moaned. Since the Americans had dropped out of the Paris Agreement program to control carbon dioxide emissions, China, India, and several other nations felt freer to continue to use coal, gas, and oil, while making a very half-hearted effort to reduce the atmospheric carbon footprint.

Speaking of footprints, we left the mighty 'Tron plodding, plowing, paddling, and pushing his way north by northwest, escaping attempts to catch him by sawing and hammering through ice (using some extra methane directed to the arms and shoulders plus some powerful manipulations from the Rana cranium/brainium to aid the prehensile hands in using tools for penetrating icy obstacles).

The layer of ice on the many lakes in Canada (Lake Winnipeg, Reindeer Lake, Great Slave Lake, and Great Bear Lake) kept Rana mostly out of sight as he moved north toward the Arctic Ocean. However, before reaching the Amundsen Gulf on the Arctic, the rootin' tootin', rapid-scootin' rugged Rana had been briefly spotted by two ice fishermen from Echo Bay on the eastern shore of the Great Bear Lake.

It was early in the morning and there was considerable fog covering the lake. The fishermen caught just a brief glimpse of some very large creature breaking through the ice at the shoreline south of Echo Bay and then rapidly descending under the ice, becoming lost from sight. Both fishermen looked at each other and inquired almost simultaneously in some mix of Canadian English, French, and Inuit: "Have we had too much to drink?" (Russian vodka was almost mandatory for their ice fishing excursions.) When they assured each other that their eyes and equilibria were passable, they climbed aboard their snowmobiles mumbling, "Baby, it's cold outside" in Anglo-Inuit, trying to locate Rana—without any success.

Even though the inhabitants of Echo Bay were interested in this nautical anomaly, they weren't sure whether the two fishermen were providing a warning or just making up some phantasmagorical fairy tale to create fear among their neighbors.

The purpose of Ranatron's trip to the Arctic was to dive to depths of about 500 meters (1,640 feet), where the temperature was low enough and the pressure of the sea water was high enough to cause the formation of frozen methane hydrates (clathrates). If a human dove deeper than 40 meters (130 feet), he would be a candidate for the bends and require decompression on returning to the surface (assuming he had no deep sea diving equipment). Rana, who didn't have lungs because the methane in his system didn't need any interaction with the atmosphere, only had to be concerned with the extreme pressure at the 500-meter depth (approximately 725 psi). The auxiliary power pump that could be filled with heated methane would allow Rana to keep his muscular legs moving. This movement could also be assisted by filling the impermeable carbon-steel-lined outer shell around his legs with a viscous fluid at high pressures to counteract the force of the ocean pressure at the depths that Rana would be investigating. The encasement of the head and upper thorax was a shell of steel-carbon-tungsten alloy that was stronger than most alloys on Earth and sufficient to keep the upper head and torso of Rana in working condition.

In his many stops (and hops) to get under the winter ice of the Canadian lakes, Rana was informed by the Ganymede gang of scientists via his reigning brain that he'd have to make use of the two cryogenic methane containers that he'd been lugging since his encounter with the Synfuels Plant in Beulah, ND. Each tank could give him about two to three months of hopping and skipping, and maybe half that amount of time if he conducted extensive dives below the icy lakes or oceans.

Rana's vertical leap was just a bit over twenty feet and his horizontal stride about 150 feet (half a football field). His swimming distance was limited by the amount of work his legs had to do. At a leisurely pace he could go about three-quarters of an hour before resting for five to ten minutes. In a sprint it would be closer to fifteen to twenty minutes. Either pace would usually be enough for him to get to some safe hiding place or escape from anyone attempting to capture him. Out of the lakes and oceans he was more vulnerable, but still not easily corralled or captured.

The closest encounter the Ranatron had to deal with was after he took an underwater look at the Great Bear Lake shoreline to see if there were any frozen methane deposits where the scout planes noted higher concentrations of methane on their chromatographic analyses. Being engrossed in his subsurface shoreline searching, he didn't notice a group of motorcyclists who had stopped at the eastern region of the lake for a rest on their trek from Yellowknife to Fort McPherson in Yukon Territory.

The bikers had hunters and fishermen in their group, and when they spotted this ferocious looking hulk emerging from the icy lake, they grabbed their Remington 753 and Mossberg Patriot deer rifles. As the startled Ranatron dove for deeper water, one of the shots from the bikers nicked his large right foot. This caused a slow leak of methane, which was critically important for the functioning of his muscles and ligaments, and thus his ability to make large and long jumps. Rana's equally powerful computer brain was able to calculate the rate of the slow leakage. Fortunately, he had a small supply of emergency polyethylene patches needed to staunch the methanic flow, since the IXonians had anticipated this need. On the side of Rana's chest, they sutured a waterproof pocket that could hold his small supply of patches.

The picnicking bikers made several runs over the frozen Great Bear Lake, but Rana had gone deep enough and made his way northeast up the Dease Arm of the lake and skirted around Fort Confidence (built in 1837 by the Hudson Bay Colony and destroyed by fire in 1911). Chimney fragments were all that remained. This fort had been located just north of the Arctic

Circle. Guided by the internal compass in his computer head, Rana traveled farther north, past Grizzly Bear Mountain, and over the barren tundra to the coast of the Arctic Ocean.

In spite of the fact that Rana's big foot injury was not too severe, and that the outflow of methane was being controlled with the patches, the 'Tron still had considerable pain when he had to push off hard in a jump or on a fast swim underwater. (The animal portion of the Randroid—the lower body, legs, and to a lesser degree, arms—had live muscles, tendons, and sensory nerves.)

After Rana had escaped from Great Bear Lake, it appeared that the rifle-toting picnickers were no longer pursuing him. He received a message from the Ganymede gurus who were monitoring his progress via almost continuous radio communication with Rana's super brain. Their instructions were for him to get out of the water for a while and see how the inflammation in his foot responded—and to see whether he had just a small infection or something more serious.

There were no Earth-type antibiotics on IXon, but the IXonians had used some of the adulterated methane from the lakes on Saturn's moon, Titan, to kill many of the infectious organisms that occurred on Planet IXon. The Titan methane contained copper contamination, which created some toxic forms of acetylene. If ignited, this could turn into a fiery explosion. But by itself, the copper was quite effective in eliminating any number of infectious species on IXon.

It was now mid-February and the weather, even in northern Canada, was relatively mild, thanks to the continual progression of global warming. This warmth allowed some patches of the tundra to be free of ice and snow and also allowed the appearance of some *Clostridium* bacteria that could cause tetanus (a.k.a. lockjaw), which could lead to severe muscle spasms and possibly death in humans. Rana didn't have to worry about lockjaw in his mechanical head and neck construction, but *Clostridium tetani* could wreak havoc on his muscles and tendons.

Without having any way to know if or what might be causing his foot to be infected, the IXon medical team felt that the best (only?) choice was to have a scout plane pilot descend close enough to lower a large container of the methane-copper-acetylene mixture and tell Rana, "Go soak your foot" (spoken in IXonese, of course). The designated drop-off site was along the northern shore of the Northwest Territories, east of Paulotuk. The delivery of the methane-copper-acetylene solution went smoothly, but the takeoff from the Amundsen Gulf by the scout plane created a fiery roar that was witnessed by a handful of native Inuits in the nearby hamlet of Paulotuk. With so many recent reports of strange objects in the sky, the word spread quickly to the Royal Canadian Mounted Police from the G Division (Northwest Territories), who could only find a couple of large web-footed prints that had not yet been washed away. There was a small melted area in the Amundsen Gulf ice where Rana slipped under the thinning ice, having had just enough time to administer an infusion of the potent gassy mixture into his foot before the Inuit or the Mounties could find him. Even though it took a while for the scout plane to find Ranatron's exact location, its ability to hover over the shore (and lower the treatment container within Rana's reach without having to land), made it much easier for the plane to get away quickly and avoid being seen.

Chapter 4

W ithin a week, the infection cleared up. With no residual damage to his foot or leg, the big 'Tron was ready to search anywhere (or maybe everywhere) on Earth for an uncontaminated form of methane.

The year on Earth was now 2036, and the world was getting warmer faster. The efforts to control climate change had been severely compromised back in 2017 by President Donald Trump. Amid many public outcries—"Dump the Trump," "Don Begone!" "Trump's a Lump" (of coal)—he decided to curtail carbon dioxide control efforts by getting out of the Paris Agreement. He also vowed to bolster the American coal mining industry. India and China eventually followed suit ("We can't let America get ahead of us!"), and the Earth's inhabitants watched the thermometer and the CO_2 levels climb steadily.

With most of the nations around the world watching what Trump and the Americans were (not) doing about global warming, the world was growing warmer in terms of meteorology, and hotter in terms of international discontent and distrust. The European Union was beginning to break up as England embarked on its Brexit. Germany and France were content to let Trump play the chump (while Germany grew more powerful than the USA) and have him be hoisted on his own petard, or fall on his own sword, or slip on a giant banana peel.

South Korea and Japan hunkered down expecting nuclear attacks from North Korea. India readied for one more assault from Pakistan. Russia's Putin was continuing his efforts to rebuild Russia to its former USSR strength by moving beyond attacking (and attaching) Ukraine and encroaching on the Baltic countries (Estonia, Latvia, Lithuania). Putin had some patronizing words for his American presidential friend (suspected business associate, sycophant). Many people (probably including Putin) felt *THE* Donald was a boor and an ignorant loudmouth.

With all this uncertainty swirling around, not many nations were paying attention to the new Bigfoot brouhaha except some Canadians and Midwestern Americans. The one aspect of the Ranatron story that was gaining more attention was the increased awareness that more "flying saucers" were being seen.

The Americans had some fast moving pursuit planes that might be mistaken for flying saucers, if seen during the nighttime hours. Iran, suffering from some reapplied sanctions, was conducting night flights, looking for possible targets to raid that might ease the bite of their economic slowdown. The long protracted battle against ISIS continued to take up much of the world's attention, and "flying saucers" were about the only thing the Jihadists couldn't be blamed for.

Rana, with the infection cleared in his foot and some additional methane given to replace the amount that had leaked from his infected foot, was now ready to resume his search for

Earth's methane. The strength in his leg was back very close to normal, so he could once again dive 500 meters.

The IXonians still didn't have an efficient device or piece of equipment that one individual could use to collect gaseous methane, and they didn't (yet) want to risk a conflict with the Earthlings by invading their territory with several hundred gas-collecting aero-tanks. Having realized that much of the methane was in the many frozen clathrate deposits, they felt they could wait until Rana had surveyed as many deposits as possible. The methane from these deposits could be mined and carried away to Ganymede and beyond much easier than the gaseous methane could be gathered and transported. However, if there were enough gaseous clouds of methane accumulating in the atmosphere, the Ganymedeans could improve their gas-collecting aero-tankers to attempt to collect the gaseous methane as well.

Earth dwellers still didn't know who or what this fabulous (fictitious?) frog-footed phantom really was, but somebody or some creature had been diving and apparently disturbing the deposits of icy methane below the surface along the Arctic Ocean shores around the Amundsen Gulf. While the Royal Canadian Mounties were snooping around on the beach and sending visual and auditory probes beneath the ice around the gulf, Rana spotted a river tributary that emptied into the ocean. He traipsed along the stream inland, careful to keep his large feet in the water that was moving fast enough to quickly obscure his tracks.

About a mile inland, the 'Tron, with his super acute hearing apparatus, began to pick up some music from a small shack not far from the bank of the stream. A seventy-eight-year-old man was playing an old forty-five-rpm vinyl record on a 1950s record player: *Lazy River* sung by the Mills Brothers. The lyrics were unintelligible to Rana, but the melody seemed to be quite pleasing, and Rana raised himself to his full eight-foot height and did a little jig in the shallow water.

Akiak Annakpok (Inuit for Brave Free) had just polished off a few beers and laughed at himself for seeing such a silly mirage bouncing around in the stream outside his cabin. He certainly had no intention of revealing anything about his mirage to the Mounties or anybody else for that matter. Even without any report from Akiak, the Mounted Police, with their widening dragnet, had most of the Northwest Territories watchful and on edge.

The Ganymede guardians became aware of the disturbance in the Northwest Territories and the Amundsen Gulf and of the searches being carried out by the Canadian police. They decided it would be best to relocate Rana a significant distance from Canada and the Arctic Ocean. There were regions in the northern Atlantic where the scout planes had obtained chromatographic evidence of methane in the air and in the Atlantic Ocean north of Iceland in the Greenland and Norwegian Seas. The fact that there were very few humans in that area made it a possible site for the Ranatron to investigate without attracting too much attention. There was some disagreement among the computerized masterminds at the Ganymede station, but they finally agreed that the 'Tron should move—or be moved—to a part of this new world where there might be other significant sources of methane.

Again, not wanting to attract too much attention, the Ganymedeans decided to pick up Rana in the Arctic Ocean area and transport him away from the police and other prying eyes. There had been considerable interest in the Black Sea, but that large body of water is situated between Russia, Turkey, and Western Europe. "Too many people," was the judgment of the IXon scientists. A better idea was to look at some of the British Isles such as Shetland, the Orkneys, and Northern Scotland where they hoped the Canadian and USA furor over Rana Superfoot had not caught on.

The pickup of Rana was again made without the scout craft having to land. The descending ladder from the scout was magnetized so that Rana, with the strong metal-fibrous digits on his prehensile hands, only had to grasp the lower rung of the lengthy ladder, which was sturdy enough to lift the big Ranatron securely and make the brief two-hour flight from the Arctic shore to the northern Atlantic Orkney Islands (situated north of Scotland and south of the Shetland Isles). The IXonian brain trust felt that Rana could do his oceanic swimming-exploration around the Orkneys and then proceed north to the Shetlands or south to the Scottish mainland—hopefully this would not attract much attention, especially if he were underwater most of the time while in these sparsely populated areas.

Rana had a full month (Earth time) before he would need another methane infusion to keep the strength and the spring in his legs at a high level. The wound in his foot had healed quite well and the new patch prevented any further leakage of the methane from his "'Tronstrous" body.

Rana was released from his magnetized scout ladder at 2 a.m. on February 29, 2036. The Orkney temperature was moderated in winter and summer by the closeness of the Gulf Stream. There were occasional snowstorms and very strong winds over the islands, but more commonly, there would be a heavy, damp fog. This foggy weather was called Haar in

Scottish parlance. All of this weather was helpful in providing cover for the inscrutable, immutable 'Tron. The IXonians always seemed to be grateful for a f(r)oggy day (or a bad *Haar* day?) to keep their Frogatron out of sight.

There were a fair number of methane clathrates along the shorelines of the Shetland and Orkney isles, but at the approximate 500-meter depth that Rana was able to dive to, there seemed to be fewer frozen stores of methane than Rana had observed around the shores of the Arctic Ocean. This may have been due to the warming effect of the Gulf Stream, but the IXonians had not yet had a chance to analyze all the patterns of the thermohaline circulations (like the Gulf Stream) around the world.

There was an inlet in the northernmost region of Scotland that the 'Tronic brain felt was worth investigating. The large inlet was the Moray Firth, between the Northwest Highlands and the Grampian Mountains. The inlet extended inland to a long and fairly wide lake that the Scots called Loch Ness. The IXonians had no idea of the long history of the Loch Ness Monster, also known as Nessie. In recent years, most of the sightings of this "monster" were discredited, and the majority of people didn't actually believe it was a real, living being. Possibly some photographic trickery purporting to be Nessie had kept the "monster myth" going.

On a Thursday in late March, Rana took his plunge into the lake, oblivious of the scattered people and small boats in and around the lake. By this time, most of the Earthlings had been exposed to the burgeoning production of androids (Asimo— almost identical to its Japanese creator, Big Dog, Pleo the dinosaur, and many others). However, they would still likely be startled or afraid if they encountered an android as large as the Ranatron.

Chapter 5

The thought that the Ranatron would not be able to continue his methane search in areas where he was likely to be seen was countered by the big 'Tron's powerful legs that allowed him to duck underwater and move away a distance "far from the madding crowd" (as in Thomas Hardy's title, in which "madding" signifies "frenzied"). This escape ability was startlingly reversed when Rana made his way southward through the Moray Firth and into the long Loch Ness.

It was now late April and many of the residents in the north of Scotland were manning their small sailboats, motorboats, or canoes and finding places along the banks of the lengthy Loch where they could enjoy a leisurely picnic. It wasn't really like the "old days" when almost everyone brought along a camera and hoped to get a picture of Nessie.

When Rana stuck his computer-mechanical head above the surface to catch a glimpse of who, what, and where these boats and boaters were going, he was greeted by gasps, gulps, and guffaws. When some of the locals, who missed the brief appearance of Rana, heard of the sighting of this strange creature, their reply was often: "Yer bum's oot the windae!"

Loosely translated, it was something like, "You're plumb out of your mind!"

The general agreement of the witnesses on Loch Ness was: "Somebody is trying to stir up another 'Nessie' story in order to get some big publicity (and a lot of money!) by increasing tourism." They also posed the question: "Who's behind this 'New Nessie' noise?"

The local authorities in the northern Scotland region felt there was no great hurry in pursuing the "likely" publicity seeker. After all, there had been no evidence of any damage done by this "New Nessie" so far.

Things started to change when the Ranatron began taking deep dives to the bottom or near bottom of the Loch where there had been an increase in the elusion of methane from the frozen clathrate deposits—partly due to global warming, but significantly increased by the Rana's intrusive dives. The additional methane entering the atmosphere was not severely toxic, but there were sufficient quantities to cause many respiratory irritations and some infections among the residents of northern Scotland and many of the tourists. And of course methane, a greenhouse gas more potent than carbon dioxide, was also adding to the Earth's global warming.

As the runaway (run amok?) Ranatron was assessing the availability and the amount of alkanes (methane, butane, octane, ethane, etc.), there was a violent thunderstorm that occurred on a late Friday night into Saturday morning. This spectacular storm had repeated bolts of lightening over most of northern Scottish territory. The lightening strikes ignited the atmosphere that now had a large amount of the alkanes (especially methane). Large portions of the northern Scottish land were affected—trees, houses, and many hundreds of humans and animals received severe burns. At this point, the fire and police departments became very involved in searching for the cause of this conflagration.

By the time the authorities realized that the sudden explosive fires set off by the thunderstorm were related to a large outpouring of natural gas (mostly methane), they began wondering if, somehow, the sighting of the "New Nessie" could be responsible in some way. "We were so sure this was some sort of ruse cooked up by some attention-seekers. We didn't pay any attention to the possibility that this strange 'thing' might've started to loosen the submerged methane clathrates and dramatically increase methane in the atmosphere," the police chief offered.

The search was on for the New Nessie/Ranatron. Rana had been heading south—for the most part beneath the lengthy Loch Ness. That was the same direction the Scottish military and police forces were also taking. At this time of year there was no snow to show any frog tracks if he had traveled a little inland from the shore. And there were no tracks in the mud until he reached the outskirts of Fort William, just south of the lake. From there he proceeded toward the Isle of Tiree.

This small island was located in the Inner Hebrides not far from the channels separating the Inner and the Outer Hebrides. These waterways were called Minch and Little Minch where the Scottish residents believed lived the Blue Men of the Minch, who were human-sized but of blue color and were responsible for sinking ships and creating storms. They supposedly swam with their torsos above water, and only dove below the water periodically. The Blue Men were also known as Kelpies (water spirits), which is also the name of some sheep dogs bred in Australia by mating the collie and the wild dingo. (In Scotland waterways, I'd stick with the water spirits.) The Blue Men were a fixture in the mythology of Northern Scotland.

A few fishermen spotted the Ranatron as it partially emerged from the ocean to approach the rocky shore of the western portion of the Isle of Tiree. The fishermen were far enough from Rana that they could only discern the strange upper body rising and then diving below the surface of the ocean. "Must have been one of the Blue Men," the fishermen surmised, but they declined to get any closer for fear of being capsized by one of the Blues brothers.

Rana waited until after midnight to climb up on the rocky shore—far enough away from the houses populating Tiree so as not to be seen. The Ranatron was quite aware of the furor it had created on the Loch Ness, and the signal was once again sent out to one of the "flying saucers" (IXon scout planes) to fly over Tiree and lift the Big Fella up by the same ladder that enabled him to escape from the Arctic Ocean shores.

Entirely unrelated to the Ranatron stirring up the methane deposits and the subsequent firestorm caused when the lightening ignited the methane-laden atmosphere, there were two milder, but significant, outbursts of fire over Lake Baikal near Irkutsk in southern Siberia. The methane gas from the lake (and some from the melting permafrost) had accumulated with the methane already in the atmosphere from human activities such as coal mining, oil and natural gas systems, agricultural activities, and landfills. As had happened in Scotland, lightening ignited the methane.

Another significant result of the outpouring of methane and other alkanes was not a firestorm, but once again multiple complaints of respiratory and sinus irritations and infections in the populace around the Caspian Sea, and extending into areas of Russia, Kazakhstan, Turkmenistan, and even into Iran.

After spending hours reviewing all the (mostly blurry) photographs of the fast-fleeting "flying saucers" and the reports of the new (and now dangerous?) Big Frog Foot, the defense forces from around the world began communicating with each other—hesitatingly at first, especially when the USA and Russia had to shelve their longstanding enmity, and when America's dubious relationships with China and Iran did not produce any warm welcoming help. The fires and choking gases appeared to be coming from some suspicious (alien?) source rather than any natural phenomena. After two to three months of head scratching and questioning, the concerned countries decided upon a worldwide conference via global television. After all the nations raised questions and double-checked sources, they reached an agreement that all Earth dwellers should join hands and try to chase down and capture one or more of the suspicious "saucers" and certainly double the efforts to track down this bizarre frog-legged creature—if, in fact, this wasn't a grand hoax.

A few countries were not on board with the idea that this was some sort of alien attack, and they were not willing to join with many of their long-time enemies. Iran, Iraq, and the shattered remains of Syria, along with several other Muslim nations, did not appear willing at any time to assist in the search. On the other hand, North Korea, not wanting to lose the reputation of being one of the world's most powerful countries, finally agreed to partake.

Saudi Arabia agreed to help fund an international network of planes, rockets, radar, lasers, and drones (unmanned aerial vehicles—UAVs). Through varying degrees of belief, the

Earth's countries gradually accepted that this was not a wild goose (or frog) chase.

The IXonians wanted to get Rana back—the single successful android that IXon scientists had constructed after many trials—especially since there was a diminishing, if not vanishing supply of large frogs back in the research facilities on IXon (due to an undiagnosed disease?). Certainly none of the recent experimental frogs even approached the size of the anomalous Rana.

While the IXonians were concentrating on the whereabouts of their Ranatron, the increasing numbers of drones circulating over most of the populated areas of the world had not seen any more of Rana since he appeared as the faux Nessie in the Loch Ness. The drones, still no match for the speed and evasiveness of the IXon scout planes, spread out over most of the populated regions of the world. Not having seen any "saucers" over Antarctica and the South Pole on all their radars, they didn't venture that far south. This led the IXonians to think it might be safe to investigate this area before having to extract Ranatron and return him to the safety of Ganymede and then back home to IXon.

In spite of the enlarging drone zone, an IXon scout plane avoided detection and successfully accomplished a middle-of-the-night pickup of Rana at the southern tip of the Barra Isles in the Outer Hebrides, northwest of Scotland. The big 'Tron was whisked away to Dronning (pronounced drawning) Maud Land (Norwegian for Queen Maud Land). Scandinavian research centers were located there, and it wasn't too long before the researchers began to notice some strange tracks—especially near the Norwegian research center (named "Troll,"

Scandinavian folklore for underground supernatural beings, either giants or little persons, living in caves).

One afternoon a Norwegian meteorologist wandered toward the northern shore of Dronning Maud Land where he saw some soft snow with two of Rana's huge frog prints. "*Hva djevelen disse sporene?*" ("What the devil are these tracks?") he muttered to himself. He had heard some of the stories from Scotland, and he wondered if Nessie had sprouted wings or if the Blue Men were looking for a new cold-water home—or perhaps the Norwegian Trolls were just wandering around.

The Ranatron broke through some of the ice floe with his powerful hands and metallic-fibrous fingers. Then with his penetrating IXonian spectrometer, he obtained a sample and a reading disclosing that these methane clathrates were even deeper than the 500-meter depth found around the Arctic and Northern Atlantic littoral shelves. It also appeared that the methane here had fewer impurities than that in the lakes of Titan and in Saturn's atmosphere. Ranatron quickly relayed the presence of these super caches of methane to the IXonian base on Ganymede. He also informed them that the Earthlings' drones and planes were beginning to come in droves in many places and that all of this activity was creating a worry for him, despite his ability to dive and disappear for long periods of time. His being in the Antarctic was, so far, not an immediate danger, but it began to look like the big 'Tron might best be taken back to the safety of Ganymede.

"We'll send a few more armed scout rocket-planes to assure that you can get out safely," the Ganymede group offered.

And so the Earth's air defense heated up, along with the ever-increasing global warming. The heightened defense alert was coordinated through NATO and a few other nations, with

China, Russia, and the Islamic countries giving at least lip service to joining the defensive and investigative forces. There was still much international debate about the origin and authenticity of this "alien attack."

The IXonian rescue rocket-plane had the power and ability to hover and execute a vertical take off and landing (VTOL). After it descended and successfully dropped Rana off on the vast Antarctic region of Dronning Maud Land, it took a bit of time to locate the Ranatron. Rana had moved west to get farther away from the research outposts of the Norwegians, the Japanese, and others. He reached the shore of the Weddell Sea, somewhere between the Halley and Georg Von Neumayer research stations (belonging to Britain and Germany, respectively). With the Earth's air and ground forces being on the alert for a big, web-footed alien, Rana did not want to radio his position for fear of giving away his location.

The scout planes managed to supply Rana with methane on a two- to three-month basis, so his legs remained powerful and in good working order. He maneuvered slowly toward an uninhabited stretch of the icy shore where he hoped a rescue scout would quickly spot him.

Fortunately, the IXon scout was able to find Rana before anyone else did. But this would not be an easy transfer. Strong winds had been gathering. The ladder rescue became impossible. The rescue rocket-plane would have to attempt a landing on the uneven, broken, icy terrain on the shore of the Weddell Sea off the northwest coast of Antarctica.

The number of Earth UAVs (drones) sent out by several countries had increased dramatically. They were now making their way south to investigate the Southern Hemisphere since they had lost track of the Ranatron in their search of the northern Hebrides isles and Scotland.

The IXon scout was beginning to pick up some drone presence on its radar, and felt it had to attempt the icy-rocky rescue as soon as possible. The freezing temperatures and almost blizzard conditions resulted in a crash landing of the scout plane on June 26, 2036. The research facilities at the British (Halley) and the Argentine (Belgrans II) stations recorded the explosion of the IXon rescue attempt on the northwest region of Antarctica known as Coats Land.

Investigating crews from the two Antarctic research centers were able to reach the crash site. They were completely surprised to find this strange airship with advanced rocket engines and VTOL capability. It was partially broken up from a fiery crash, and there was evidence of methane in the ice and snow that hadn't been totally consumed. Even more surprising was the mangled form of the totally robotic pilot, along with the equally mangled sophisticated apparatus that could send and receive messages. The mechanical computer brain of this robot was not as large as most of the computers on Earth, but apparently it could be a match for the ninety-three petaFLOPS Sunway supercomputer made by the Chinese—smaller, but just as powerful—or more so. Parts of the IXon scout plane were damaged badly enough that it would take the Earth's scientists and technicians a long time to try to unravel all its mysteries.

The other notable findings were the large frog prints that led to the icy shore of the Weddell Sea. The runaway Rana had taken a dive into the frigid Weddell Sea the moment he saw his rescue plane crash. He navigated through some ice and a few icebergs that had calved away from the Antarctic Dotson and Crosson Ice Shelves—part of global warming and melting. He made his way toward the Antarctic Peninsula which formed a curve angling from the west in a more northeasterly direction—about 800 miles to Cape Horn at the southern end of South America.

The main problem Rana now confronted was the expenditure of a great deal of his methane supply, which was going to his legs, his muscle-metal arms, and the separate heating mechanism that operated with his thermostat to keep the muscles warm and functioning at a high level. Furthermore, the eyes and guns of the world were collecting in the region of the Falkland Islands (where the British and Argentinians battled in 1982) and Tierra del Fuego (Land of Fire) at the southern tip of South America, where they assumed this strange "alien" might be headed.

Chapter 6

With his reserve supply of methane having gone up in a fiery explosion along with the IXon scout, Rana made his way slowly and cautiously to Berkner Island off the coast of Antarctica—a significant distance from where the scout had crashed, and part way to the Antarctic Peninsula. It was necessary to keep moving as quickly as possibly so as not to be spotted and trapped by the increasing number of drones, planes, and research personnel on the peninsula. This did not allow him to spend any time drilling along the area of the Larsen ice shelves where there might be plenty of methane from many available clathrates. Again, Rana hesitated to send any signals to the scout planes for fear of giving away his own, or their, locations.

On the other hand, a few of the scouts were able to beam their low frequency radar onto the icy caves that were scattered around the peninsula, and Scout-One did determine the cave where the Frogatron was hiding and decided to make a dive toward his position. What seemed like an unopposed approach to the ice cave was interrupted by two armed American drones, which immediately opened fire on the IXon Scout-One. The speed and quick maneuverability of the scout allowed it to avoid getting hit, and the IXonian returned fire with its laser-guided canons, which had superior guidance and firing mechanisms as compared to the Earth drones. The two drones were quickly eliminated.

After the smoke cleared, Scout-One radioed to Scout-Three, which was carrying supplies of liquid methane that could sustain Rana. "Scout-Three, can you drop the methane transport container close to Rana's ice cave before more drones come bearing down on this icy location?"

Scout-Three dropped the heavy methane tank within a couple hundred yards of the cave. The 'Tron risked being seen by quickly running and jumping—in about six giant strides—to retrieve the precious methane. On his way back to the cave he attempted to cover his web-footed tracks. He apparently did a good enough job because when more drones flew over to assess the damage to the downed drones—over a mile away from the Rana cave—they saw nothing of the Ranatron's hideout or footprints. When the coast was clear, Rana, with his new infusion of methane, figured he should be moving on.

A sidelight to the explosive, fiery destruction of the two Earth drones several hours earlier was how the fusillade from the IXon scouts had disrupted and penetrated a large segment of the frozen shore on the edge of the Weddell Sea. This exposed a large body of the frozen clathrates that resided beneath the ice.

The power and speed of the IXon missiles were considerably greater than any of the Earthling armamentarium, and consequently could penetrate far deeper beneath the ice/water surface. The clathrates burst into flames, despite their frozen nature (the methane was that powerful of an ignitable substance).

The Earthlings were both challenged and significantly concerned because of the fact that the two American drones were quickly destroyed by these better-performing alien flyers. They hoped that their Earth forces were in large enough numbers to surround and overwhelm their fast-moving foe.

The first wave of drones, joined by fighter jets, approached the region around southern South America. The powerfully armed alien IXon scouts scattered and retreated toward the mid-Pacific Ocean where their methane-supplying aerial tankers could rapidly refuel their aircraft in midair. The Earth's drones and fighters were busy concentrating their efforts over as many land and populated areas around southern South America as possible—where they presumed the Frogatron and the armed scouts might be heading and possibly creating more havoc.

After the IXon Scouts Two and Six were refueled, the pilots deemed it wiser to stay away from the drone-infested areas around South America. The few new arrivals of scouts from Ganymede, which had been constructed with heavier armament, would be better suited to pursue the Ranatron.

Earth intelligence still didn't know Rana's course. Many of the Earth's drone operators and jet pilots figured the 'Tron might be headed toward South Georgia & the South Sandwich Islands or the Falkland Islands on the Atlantic side of South America. In the meantime, IXons Two and Six were moving from their refueling locations over the mid-Pacific back toward the California coast where their duties were to patrol the west coast of the USA all the way from Washington State to southern California.

Over northern California, the rapidly darting IXon fighter scouts unexpectedly encountered a couple of drones that had been sent to patrol the west coast to uncover any alien activity. More drones were to join them shortly as part of the Earth's expanded defense program. Realizing that they would have to fight their way out of some web of drones eventually, IXons Two and Six began firing their streamlined bullet/grenade/mini bombs. These munitions were an advanced form of tungsten-based reactive metal that would explode on contact. This innovative explosive was similar to what the Americans and other countries had been working on for years.

When these bullet/grenades hit their target, they would explode and create a firestorm of damage. What the IXonians hadn't considered was what would happen when these exploding weapons would miss the targeted drones and hit the land or sea instead. Explosions on land would likely create a great deal of fire damage, but nothing compared to the shots that penetrated the oceans. They would mostly go deep along the shorelines where the water was getting saturated with natural gases—especially methane—thanks to global warming, which was causing the clathrates to slowly melt and release the gases. If any of these air battles took place over areas of the far northern tundra, the release of natural gas would also explode into a fireball.

What began as localized battles along the western United States and around the Antarctic Ocean very quickly extended to other areas around the globe. This widespread immolation not only created more fires, but severely affected the atmosphere over large regions and persisted long enough to cause millions of deaths to humans as well as to much of the fauna and flora.

The IXonians realized from their chromatographic surveys, as well as the Ranatron's suboceanic forays, that the methane hydrate deposits all around the globe were very large (multiple tons). The Arctic and Antarctic regions were especially rich in these deposits. As global warming increased, and many countries still refused to limit their carbon emissions, the previously frozen tundra began releasing methane from the land as well as the seas.

When the amount of damage along the California coast was analyzed, it appeared that the explosive bullets/grenades/small bombs had unleashed a torrent of methane gas that was partially enclosed in a watery cloud, and that began to blow eastward from California on the predominant winds from the West (westerlies). Crops and people were caught in these gusts of methane clouds, and the city of Sacramento had to slow down their operations and have many of their inhabitants move quickly north or south out of the path of these stifling clouds, which could be explosive when any sort of fire or lightening ignited them.

The brain trust of IXon began to realize that the hammering by all their munitions along the shorelines—especially in the far north and far south—could release huge amounts of methane gas. Their special suction-receptacle flying tanks, which they had perfected for their atmospheric collections over Titan and Saturn, could then collect the methane gas. With the realization that so much methane was contained on Earth, the IXonians felt that it might be quite feasible to not only create a chaotic scene throughout the world, and thereby more easily rescue their super Ranatron, but also possibly collect a lot more of Earth's relatively pure methane.

They had estimated that even allowing for the substantial amount of gaseous methane that was escaping to the atmosphere (from global warming and the disruption of the methane clathrates), there would still be plenty that could be both collected with their aerial retrieval system and harvested from the tons of submerged clathrates.

Could the IXonians stun the Earthlings, and probably eliminate millions of them with multiple clouds of methane gas? The answer came suddenly when multiple summer thunderstorms occurred in the Northern Hemisphere. Lightening flashes began setting off firestorms, especially along the coastlines, limiting the available methane that could be salvaged by the IXonians.

The bombardment of the shorelines by the IXon air forces in several locations was augmented by the increased offshore drilling for oil reserves that many nations had begun in order to bolster the dwindling oil and gas reserves worldwide. This drilling, in a number of places, was responsible for more disruption of the subsurface methane hydrate. The vibratory force of the drilling, occasionally leading to earthquakes, was just one more factor in the release of methane from the clathrates.

During the summer months, the hot weather led to large clouds supersaturated with methane gas. Many cities were almost paralyzed by the choking gas and the widely destructive fires that accompanied lightening strikes. The rapid and elusive IXonian fighter scouts lost a couple of their planes, but nowhere near the number of drones and fighters that Earth lost.

The IXonians' original plan was to have their mega Ranatron search for any methane supplies on this Blue Planet, but when they saw the major disturbance this made and they had to send in their armed scout planes to rescue Rana, they realized how devastating their attacks had been against the slower, less maneuverable Earthlings. Some IXonians felt that they could take over this planet and avail themselves of this purer (than Titan's) methane. If they planned to make Earth a permanent satellite of IXon, however, they had not calculated how much of the Earth's methane would still be available after all the disruption of the clathrate beds, nor how to survive in a very polluted oxygen environment.

Through all the furious fighting, exploding, and huge firestorms, Rana had hunkered down in a cave on an unoccupied islet southwest of the tip of South America and was awaiting some signal from Ganymede's air force of when it would be safe to move on or whether to wait to be picked up by another scout plane.

Chapter 7

As the methane clouds plus the lightening storms began moving east, and the devastating attacks by the IXon rocket-planes seemed to be increasing, the government in Washington, DC began dispersing into hideouts in the hills of Virginia and West Virginia—some of which had been around since the Cold War between the USA and Russia. Both Russia and China had not been in the main areas of conflict with the alien fighter scouts, although they both sent token numbers of planes and a few UAVs to help bolster the fighters against the aliens. The real design of both China and Russia was to finally see the USA get shut down since they appeared to be hardest hit by these aliens and some giant Frogenstein nonsense.

Over the past twenty-plus years, China's economy had flourished while the United States' seemed to be sinking slowly. The embarrassing know-nothing, do-nothing president Trump had been impeached for not only his *non compos mentis*, but also for his documented collusion with the Russians over shady financial deals, and his attempts to influence the American presidential election of 2016 and to further damage the reputation of his opponent Hillary Clinton. Meanwhile president Putin of Russia had a hearty laugh and continued to try to reconstruct a more powerful Russia by moving in on the Baltic states (Estonia, Latvia, Lithuania) after walking all over Ukraine. In addition to the Trump travails, the US Congress managed to conduct a perfect performance of an unarmed civil war—Republicans vs. Democrats, propose and deny—and accomplish nothing!

Earth dwellers still knew very little about Planet IXon. Only recently could their superior telescopes track some of the flights that were leaving the suspected location of IXon and heading for Ganymede. At the early stages of the alien encounters, they still weren't clear about the origin or functioning of the semi-mythical Ranatron.

The battle between the IXonians and the Earthlings continued for years. It was still not clear whether the technical superiority of the relatively small fleet of IXon fighter scouts was going to be able to win out over the superior numbers of the slower, but still potentially dangerous, drones and fighter planes of the Earth's air force.

Extracting the precious Ranatron had been quite difficult, until the air battle shifted back toward North America. The majority of the IXonians moved away from South America to allow IXon Six better access to *Señor Gigantas Ancas de Rana* (giant frog legs), as they would say in Argentina. This allowed an easier pickup and extraction of Rana from the small island where he had taken refuge. It took some time to accurately find Rana's location since he was so often on the move to avoid detection by the Earthlings.

Rana's legs were getting weaker as he had expended so much energy island hopping and dodging. He used up almost all of his methane "blood," and there appeared some diminution of the size of his powerful legs. The mechanical activity of Rana's brain was also diminishing. The supposed waterproofing of the Ranatron head/brain/computer was showing signs of wear and may have needed an overhaul or at least some cleansing and a recheck of all its functions.

After the successful rescue of the weakened Ranatron, the IXon scout planes were ordered to return to Ganymede along with the Ranatron. As the scout pilots withdrew back to the base on Ganymede, they felt relieved that none of the Earthling planes and drones had the capability of covering the distance to Jupiter's largest moon, Ganymede.

What was left of the smoldering Earth? So many of the submerged methane clathrate beds had begun exploding or melting after the barrage of shots that came from both sides of the combatants. In addition to the battering around California, significant disruption of the methane beds around Australia and the Melanesian islands occurred during a major battle over the Solomon and Coral Seas.

The Earth was beginning to melt. Would the retreat of the alien forces help diminish the methane pouring out of the ocean beds and lessen the suffocating heat? Or would global warming persist, allowing the hot temperatures to continue? Even if the atmospheric conditions did not yet appear to be leading to an extinction, the persistent odor of the methane, especially when mixed with sulfur from volcanic activity and other underground sources, definitely made for an ex-*stink*-tion. It would take years, certainly, to reconstruct the cities that had been so severely damaged by fires, smothering gases, and alien aerial attacks—not to mention farms, forests, animals, etc.

All the damage done to so many of the Earthlings had a leveling effect on several of the warring nations throughout the world. The ISIS powers had to think hard about their plans to take over the world and convert multiple millions to their radical Sharia ideology. The Israelis and Palestinians began to realize that there now was a big(-ger?) and largely unknown alien enemy.

It seemed to harken back to the 1940s and '50s when suddenly many nations had to work together to fight the exploding Japanese threat (Pearl Harbor), and the Nazis who were invading Europe and Russia and trying to dominate the rest of the world.

In the case of the Methane Mess, no one knew whether this alien attack would lead to a prolonged conflict throughout the solar system—or maybe the galaxy? Nor did anyone know who or what this demi-frog was. Or what sort of advanced scientific anomaly the Earthlings might confront.

The engineers and astrophysicists on Earth had been working on building bigger and better rockets and advanced propulsion systems that might be needed for getting away from a world that appeared to be crumbling with endless wars and now the specter of a *Frogissimus maximus* and the aliens. Would there be thousands more Ranatrons? The IXon scientists had been working for a long time to create more giant frogs, which then could be combined with the advanced computer-brain in order to have a large stable of Randroids.

However, in their attempts to make mechanical robots that could leap and swim, they were unable to replicate the power and superior mobility of their one and only Ranatron. It looked like it would be years before the IXonians could create other giant frogs. The one giant Rana apparently had some genetic mutation that resulted in his gigantism. The IXonian geneticists had apparently not conquered as many of the mysteries of the genome as had the scientists on Planet Earth. However, the Earth geneticists weren't trying to produce any giants. Many ethical and biological considerations prevented invasive involvement of the embryonic stem cell germline, which might have been engineered to create super animals or super humans.

As the Run-amok Rana and all the scout planes returned to Ganymede, there was considerable debate among the IXonians as to whether or not they should return to the Blue Planet and make it an outpost satellite. Many of them believed that the fireworks that took place on Earth might have destroyed a large portion of the methane. Since the prospecting that the IXonians had done on Earth was severely limited due to the fighting, the debate continued among their leaders of whether or not to return. Those voting to return were influenced by the higher purity of the methane on Earth compared to the purity on Titan and Enceladus. The majority was in favor of continuing their research stations on Ganymede and Planet IXon but *not* returning to the belligerent Blue Planet.

At the same time, scientists and military experts, especially in the United States, were working feverishly to trace where the Ranatron and its caretakers were truly from. They noted some rockets coming from the general area where they suspected there *might be* a ninth planet far away in the Kuiper belt, but they still hadn't verified that there *was* a planet in that location, much less an inhabited planet where the space temperatures were far below what would be expected to support life. They also had absolutely no idea that this planet had great amounts of volcanic activity that could support a subterranean environment, sufficiently warm to allow a methane-dominated atmosphere where swamp creatures could flourish, and who knows how, produce a very small cluster of brilliant, small-bodied, big-brained robotic-persons who could lead this aberrant world into a science-superior nation.

In the next two decades, some of the ravages on Earth had been cleared up, but the combination of the methane still leaking out of the oceans, the never-ending global warming, and the increased activity of volcanoes and earthquakes, kept the clouds of volcanic ash, sulfur, and methane putting a strangle hold on the environment. Crops were failing, and humans and animals were suffering from a myriad of respiratory and other infections. There were still quite a few universities and scientific laboratories looking for instrumentation that could absorb the unhealthy gases and purify the air so that they could continue their research projects (and help improve the air quality in many houses and buildings in the USA and elsewhere).

Artificial intelligence (AI) research on Earth, which had been stalled due to all the global unrest, was finally getting back to where it was before the Froggy (and foggy) days of incessant methane fires and explosions. In fact, AI had progressed so far that it was rapidly approaching futurist Ray Kurzweil's "singularity"—when artificial intelligence becomes greater than human brainpower (as was nicely portrayed by Robert Colvile in his book *The Great Acceleration*). This could include amazing new phenomena such as microbots in the blood stream weeding out unwanted cancer cells.

After seeing or hearing about the powerful Ranatron, scientists and engineers put in many long hours developing a mechanical exoskeleton that would give an individual amazing amounts of strength and endurance. So far, no android had been perfected with a hopping, jumping, long-distance swimming ability such as that of the rambling Ranatron. Maybe it would just be a matter of time.

In addition to all the AI improvements, there were some major developments in the understanding of the human genome with the CRISPR-Cas9 procedure. To hopefully eliminate some life-threatening diseases, this could add and subtract genetic material to or from the genome.

All of these relatively new explorations in computer science and human biology would lead many to believe this would give Earth an edge over any foreign or alien attacks, but there were many others who worried that all of these changes might leave humanity in a lesser, secondary status—beholden to the new mechanical and biological marvels. Would AI take over the world?

Colvile's book gives the example of professor Martin Rees of England who, with several others, set up the Centre of Existential Risk and contemplated the possibility of a super plague engineered by some individual or terrorist group that could kill millions of people. Could the methane invasion be the next plague?

Chapter 8

Mike McGowan was wounded by an exploding mini bomb fired by one of the IXonian planes. McGowan had been working as a computer expert out of his office in Los Angeles. It was a Sunday morning and he was walking his dog "Terrible Tess" (she was a bit over-frisky) along the Pacific shore of Santa Barbara where he lived. The sudden appearance of the plane and the almost simultaneous explosion of the mini bomb barely gave Mike time to duck. He suffered lacerations of the left side of his head as he tried to turn away. Poor Tess got the worst of the explosion and did not survive. Mike's wife, hearing all the noise, rushed from their house, and when she saw Mike (and her beloved dog), she immediately called for an ambulance and had Mike transported to the nearest hospital.

Michael's injuries were not life threatening, but as he was recovering he had a chance to think long and hard about what the future would hold. Being an expert in computer science, he mentioned to his wife on her daily visits to the hospital about the cyberwar attacks that had taken place even before the alien-froggy invasion caused total disruption.

"Pick your poison?" his wife added with a sigh of resignation.

Michael had been doing lots of reading over the past few years. One book, *The Inevitable,* by a fellow Californian, Kevin Kelly, was about predicting future technological forces. Regarding the computer world, Kelly states that humans would be forming "a cloud of machine intelligences and then linking billions of their own minds into this single supermind [. . .] a grand network of hitherto unimagined complexity" (p. 291).

Michael wondered if this proposed super-brain could possibly be a force for good. So much of the present world had been using computers for cyber-interference (cyberwar) against other nations. Would this alien invasion from IXon possibly bring about a joining together of many nations that had been fighting war after war against each other since the ape-men climbed down from the trees? The initial response to the IXonians looked possibly promising as a binding force that might have the Earthlings pull together against this alien enemy. However, would it last after the IXon troops departed for Ganymede and beyond?

While Mike McGowan was still recuperating from his face and skull injuries he wondered how much damage had been done to Earth's methane supplies. Many of the nations around the world were hurting from the reduced supplies of gas and oil. The USA still had a substantial amount of oil and gas from fracking activities in Middle America, but the supplies in the Middle East and Asia were becoming markedly low.

Japan, India, Canada, and the United States had been experimenting with different methods of harvesting methane—which had been recognized as a possible substitute for the dwindling gas and oil reserves. Coring (digging cores), pressure reduction, and ion exchanges were some of the methods used. Multibeam Swath Sounders had come into use for locating methane clathrate concentrations by using ultrasound. However, some of the attempts to uncover the clathrate beds by the circulation of hot water pumped into the hydrates to raise the temperature (which allowed the hydrate to break down and release the methane gas) were hurried. This unloosed a great deal of methane into the air. The poorly controlled drilling, aided and abetted by global warming, resulted in more heavy methane-loaded clouds to form and spread with the wind. There was even a strategy using carbon dioxide infusions into the clathrates. The carbon dioxide would displace the methane in the clathrates, but again, care was needed to prevent even more leakage and contamination of the atmosphere.

While the Earthlings were coughing, sputtering, and putting out fires from the lightening-ignited, methane-contaminated atmosphere, there were many scientists, rocket engineers, and astronomers who were frantically trying to ascertain exactly where these aliens came from originally. They traced some of the alien flights to Ganymede and wondered how in the world they were able to get from Ganymede to Earth in such short times. It takes about 48 minutes 21.39 seconds for light to travel to Jupiter (and roughly the same for Io, Europa, Callisto, and Ganymede). The distance from Earth to Jupiter's moons was so great that it would take rockets with the top propulsion systems from the USA or Russia around *six years* to make a manned flight to Ganymede. Whatever the advanced systems were that the aliens used, the Earthlings did not understand them.

Had the aliens acquired some nuclear propulsion to power their rapid-darting scout planes? The Marshall Space Flight Center in Huntsville, Alabama had tested non-nuclear materials to simulate nuclear fuels. Active fissile material was considered too dangerous at this point in their research. The Nuclear Thermal Rocket Element Environmental Simulator (NTREES), which tested elements and materials in hot, flaming hydrogen, was still in the investigative stages. Another spacecraft propulsion device under development was the VASIMR (Variable Specific Impulse Magnetoplasma Rocket)—a plasma-ion engine using inert propellants such as argon, xenon, or hydrogen (and sometimes krypton). The rocket was projected to reach Mars in thirty-nine days—still not matching the Ganymede gang's superfast, very maneuverable, nuclear-propelled scout fighter, which could go from Earth to Ganymede in about a year.

Mike McGowan continued researching and rethinking all that had happened. He thought a lot about what he read related to where the world was and where it might be going. Before the alien frog invasion of the Earth, there was a concerted effort by many nations to perfect the art of using cyberspace as a weapon. The Chinese certainly became adept at hacking into many businesses and military facilities. The Russians used their cyber skills to attempt to influence the 2016 US presidential election. The United States and Israel developed a cyber worm (Stuxnet) that disrupted the Iranian nuclear weapons production. How far would the cyberwars go? Michael had the ominous feeling that cyberspace would be the next world war—that is, until the aliens and their giant frog came along.

Chapter 9

Even if the Frogorama circus with the aliens did not go any further, Michael also had many concerns about AI and the rapid development of robotics. There seemed to be many scientists who believed that robots and cyborgs would rapidly become smarter than humans, and possibly relegate the human race to a secondary or inferior position. However, some of the scientists and futurists like Ray Kurzweil felt that even if singularity came within the next decade, there would be many ways that humans and machines could collaborate and not be overtaken by computerized robots that could process multiple petaFLOPS of information in mere seconds.

In the 2015 book *Cyber-Humans* by Woodrow Barfield that Mike was reading, the author describes some of the optimistic ideas that Kurzweil had. He states that by the 2040s, "non-biological intelligence may be a billion times more capable than biological intelligence by linking wirelessly from our neo-cortex to a synthetic neurocortex in the 'cloud'" (p. 275). Kurzweil also felt that there would be nanobots (microscopic robots) that, by 2020, would be able to eradicate most diseases, and the nanobots would become smarter than current medical technology and self-replicate in the human body to fight disease. The scientific community seemed to be quite divided as to whether the striking advances in AI would be a major boon or a scary evolution into a non-human world.

"After what all the nations on Earth have been through, what will we face next—destruction by aliens or demotion to being pets of robots?" Michael mused. There was one other possibility that Michael hadn't considered—and it might be a real gasser!

Mike McGowan's contusions and lacerations from the alien aerial attack were viewed as non-life-threatening, but the physicians at Santa Barbara were concerned about a compression fracture of the third cervical vertebra in Mike's neck. He didn't appear to have any neurological damage, but the doctors would have to keep a close eye on this injury. Even though Mike had to wear a cervical neck brace for six to eight weeks, he was not in a great deal of pain. He would have to stay quiet at home after discharge from the hospital, and then return for frequent follow-up visits with the neurologists and orthopedists. He was actually pleased that he would have more time to continue learning about the ways of the world.

Mike, of course, was pretty well up to date on all the progress being made in the computer world. He was also quite familiar with "Moore's Law," which predicted that the power and speed of computer processing would double every eighteen to twenty-four months.

Mike's wife Molly had brought many of his books up to the bedroom so he could remain relatively still and not have to worry about slipping and falling. One of the books, *Wired for War* by P.W. Singer (2009), had an interesting quote from Einstein: "Never attribute to malice that which can be adequately explained by stupidity. Only two things are infinite, the universe and human stupidity, and I'm not sure about the former" (p. 434).

In discussing cyber warfare in *Wired for War*, Singer says that technology might even create a new species, but that this may be hampered by conflicts, such as those that have plagued human history. He states, "Sadly, our machines may not be the only thing wired for war" (p. 436).

"You sure got that right!" Michael murmured.

In a similar vein, James Barrat states in his 2013 book, *Our Final Invention*, that he has encountered a minority of people, including some scientists, who won't even discuss the idea of dangerous AI because they think it's not plausible. In his opinion, this does not, unfortunately, change the steady and inevitable growth of machine intelligence. He warns that if humans don't accept, explore, and monitor this threat, they may miss their chance to positively coexist with things that have a greater intelligence than them.

Just to add to Michael's concern about the future, there were some other worrisome problems besides the human-machine-singularity possibilities. Richard Haass, in his 2017 book *A World in Disarray*, states that the world is on a trajectory toward disorder, which is linked more so to structural changes in the international system than to major power conflicts of the past. He explains that the world has a multitude of decision makers and independent actors that are feeding this disorder, and that major powers can't handle the emerging global and regional challenges. These include for example, the existing and future spread of nuclear weapons, increased refugees and displaced people, a chaotic Middle East, a largely ungoverned cyberspace, inadequate attention paid to climate change, and a growing pandemic that could cause millions of deaths.

"Sounds like the world we're living in now," Michael and Molly both agreed.

"Molly, honey, could you bring me a bottle of aspirin—I don't think I want to read anymore!"

Molly brought the aspirin and carefully moved Michael's box of books out of his sight. She thought she would wait a while before she let Mike know about the fascinating book she was reading: *Scatter, Adapt and Remember (How Humans Will Survive a Mass Extinction)* by Annalee Newitz (2013). The last chapter is entitled "On Titan's Beach." (Did she know something about the methane lakes and maybe some hints about a Planet IX?) Newitz discusses how far humans have come in a million years and that in another million years they could be living on Saturn's moons Titan or Enceladus. She suggests that future technologies to make this possible will make rocket fuels and supercomputers look ancient, as tools from *Homo erectus* or *Homo habilis* look to modern humans. She says that astronomers often identify Titan as a possible place for colonization because of its thick atmosphere that could protect humans from solar radiation.

Newitz further describes how Titan has beaches with dunes, methane rainfall, lakes made of methane, and occasional volcanoes that erupt with ice. Such an environment would freeze and poison humans, but she postulates that maybe they could survive there if they had some type of lung implant that could covert gases into something that could oxygenate human blood.

Molly was especially taken by Newitz's thoughts about how future generations will only make it to Saturn's moons if they choose to work as a planet to explore the solar system rather than choose warfare. Newitz asserts that this is important because in the long term, it will take the world on a path toward survival rather than death.

Molly could almost hear her husband saying: "Amen, Annalee Newitz!—Amen!"

Newitz also relates the work that former astronaut Mae Jemison was doing on the 100 Year Starship project, the goal of which is to bring hundreds of humans to another star system. It was so named because Jemison and her colleagues estimated that it would take roughly a century to develop all the necessary technology.

Newitz muses about the next million years, posing the questions: What will our progeny remember about *Homo sapiens*? What do we want it to mean when they call themselves humans? She says she personally hopes her post-*Homo sapiens* offspring, "frolicking with their robot bodies in the lakes of Titan," will remember their ancestors as brave beings that never stopped exploring. She concludes: "Things are going to get weird. There may be horrible disasters and many lives will be lost. But don't worry. As long as we keep exploring, humanity is going to survive" (p. 263).

While Michael was still very concerned about things robotic and electronic (whose your daddy?—Tron?), wife Molly didn't have to get into a sci-fi scenario to be concerned about the future. In addition to her forays into the Annalee Newitz futurism, she was struck by the number of economists and political scientists who were seeing doom and gloom in many of America's relationships with other countries (e.g., Gideon Rachman's 2017 book *Easternization: Asia's Rise and America's Decline from Obama to Trump and Beyond* and Edward Alden's 2016 book *Failure to Adjust: How America Got Left Behind in the Global Economy*).

Graham Allison, in his 2017 book *Destined For War*, even referred back to the Peloponnesian Wars when Sparta, the major military power, was challenged by an up-and-coming Athens. Thucydides, a Greek historian (*not*, as some have believed, related to the two Athenian tailors: *Euripides* and *Eumenides*?) had developed the theory that when a powerful nation is challenged by a rising, and possibly more powerful, nation, they are in a "Thucydides Trap." Historically, such traps have ended in war when the party of the first part fears the rising power of the party of the second part—USA, party of the first—China, party of the second. War is not inevitable, but throughout history it has happened in ten of fourteen national clashes that Allison describes.

Intrigued by all these treatises on America's outlook for the future, Molly ran into *A Sinking Nation—Unraveling the Complexities of the U.S. Debt and Deficit* (2016) by Bob Marshall, CPA. She learned of the problems with the Affordable Care Act (ACA), the individual mandate that couldn't get untracked (except in Massachusetts), and how "Obama Care" had become the Un-ACA. She vowed to look into how a thriving nation like Sweden could afford single-payer universal health care, and decided not to delve into any other pessimistic tomes such as the 2016 *The Road To Ruin*: *The Global Elites' Secret Plan for the Next Financial Crisis* by James Rickards.

Chapter 10

Another unexpected release of methane occurred when California geologists and seismologists used explosive materials to investigate the pattern and extent of many of California's fault systems that could potentially result in damaging earthquakes. The explosives used in this investigation inadvertently disrupted many methane clathrates. This activity added more methane to the greenhouse gases already in the atmosphere.

The increased global warming, increase in volcanic activity in many of the northern regions of the world (e.g., Iceland), Jihadi Jingoists creating havoc, cyberattacks resulting in such things as destroyed electrical grids and stolen military schemata, never-ending wars of religion, battles to acquire territory, and the over-population of many parts of the Earth all were creating a progressive weakening—and in some cases destruction—of fauna, flora, and humanity. Plus, the choking effect of the methane clouds in combination with volcanic dust, ash, sulfur, etc. resulted in multiple thousands of subsequent respiratory infections—asthma, pneumonia, chronic obstructive pulmonary disease (COPD), lung cancer, and more.

Michael and Molly realized the atmosphere, along the California coast, was getting to be unbearable with the continued influx of methane from the alien shelling and the geological investigations. Michael's brother was living in Sacramento, which is a good distance inland from the California coast and, so far, was only minimally affected by the methane blowing from west to east from the coast.

"Time to move," Michael said, and Molly fully agreed. Mike's brother had been a geologist with the State of California, and he was able to "comfort" his brother and sister-in-law about moving, in spite of the fact that there were a few other areas that were potentially quite worrisome.

There had been an increase in earthquakes in California, but also in Mid-America—possibly as a result of fracking for shale oil and gas. The whole of Iceland, which sits on the Mid-Atlantic Ridge, has been separating due to tectonic plate movement. This could lead to a greater risk of volcanic eruption.

Iceland's 2011 Grímsvötn volcanic eruption spread ash around the world, fouling the atmosphere and severely affecting airplane activities. There were also reports that as the ice covers melted due to global warming, the volcanoes under the glaciers would explode and continue to pollute the atmosphere. Iceland also had the Katla volcano, which had been erupting about every fifty to a hundred years (the last time was in 1918). And the unpronounceable Eyjafjallajökull volcano, which last erupted in 2010, was another source of ash, sulphur, dust, and things clastic.

Now that Mike and Molly tried to incorporate all this knowledge of volcanic activity into their already deep concern about the explosive methane polluting the atmosphere, Mike's brother threw in a couple questions to consider: 1) Would the Krakatoa volcano in Indonesia repeat its 1883 eruption, which killed over 36,000 people? 2) Would the vast magma caldera under Yellowstone National Park erupt again? It had done so three times in the past—the most recent being 640,000 years ago. The volcanologists and geologists had noticed a recent increase in the elevation of the ground in areas of Yellowstone Park, but no one was ready to predict an imminent eruption. The prior three eruptions occurred roughly 600,000 years apart—so maybe it was overdue. If the Yellowstone caldera were to erupt, it would cause severe damage all across the United States, and it would add a considerable load to the already heavily laden air.

Michael and Molly McGowan and their two sons successfully made the move to Sacramento, but it wasn't long before the territory around the countryside outside of Sacramento began to look as bleak as the California coastal region they had recently left. Michael looked at the area around his brother's home in the suburbs of Sacramento and saw the ruined crops of fruits and vegetables. He watched the few straggling, emaciated cattle, which had fallen prey to the failing crops, now face starvation.

Michael recalled much of his California history—especially that of the San Fernando Valley that had survived heavy floods and prolonged droughts since the 1880s—but nothing was as prolonged and devastating as this methane madness. Of course, it wasn't just the farms or the animals that were being reduced to practically nothing. Human populations were suffering from hunger, respiratory infections, and bankruptcy. Some were evacuated eastward toward Montana, Wyoming, Arizona, and

Utah, but many didn't have the health or the wealth to leave for greener pastures.

Fortunately, Michael had been able to get work in California's capital, but his structural engineering company soon decided to move to Guadalajara, Mexico—a city of Tequila, Mariachi music, and, being the second largest city in Mexico, a large and growing number of computer and tech companies. Mexico had managed to stay out of the madcap methane battles with the aliens and their giant Frogatron.

Michael's oldest son had just finished high school and was admitted to the Monterrey Institute of Technology (Mexico's MIT?). His younger son had one more year of high school, and he and his family all struggled a bit to learn Spanish. The boys were both bright, and Alec, the younger one (sometimes referred to by his parents as the "smart" Alec), hoped to follow his big brother in getting an engineering education.

Mexico had been fortunate in avoiding the ravaging Jihadi movements, which had slowed down during the last ten years of increased heat and uncertain floods. Mexico was also fortunate to find sufficient sustenance for their widespread, wild-eyed, sabre-wielding warriors. The Jihadi intent, although slowed, was still to concentrate on the USA and Europe to hopefully take command of these and other nations, and establish their worldwide caliphate.

With the methane madness, global warming, rising oceans, and failing crops, the Jihadi Jingoist attempts at world domination were waning further. Was this truly the beginning of the sixth major extinction? How similar was this situation to the disruption on Earth sixty-six million years ago when a huge asteroid slammed into Mexico near the town of Chicxulub? That, along with prolonged volcanic activity worldwide, had created so much pollution in the atmosphere that it was associated with the extinction of the dinosaurs. Small mammals did survive—and eventually evolved into human beings.

There had been a few non-extinction occurrences in the world that also caused considerable difficulties to the humans on Earth. One was the Little Ice Age (about 1600 to 1850 CE), possibly caused by cyclical lows in solar radiation, heightened volcanic activity (especially the Tambora eruption), changes in ocean circulation, variation in Earth's orbit, and tilting of the Earth on its axis. It even snowed in New England in July 1816.

Unrelated to the Little Ice Age, there was also "The Great Famine" in 1315 to 1322. The causes are uncertain, but this led to extreme numbers of deaths, even cannibalism and infanticide. Could any of the present woeful conditions on Earth be short (and possibly agonizing) years, but like in the past, followed by recovery? Even the Great Plague of 1348 to 1375 was survivable despite millions of deaths. Where was Earth headed?

How long would the methane eruptions continue, and how long would the life-threatening atmosphere continue to exist? Methane gas, by itself, can rise more easily and more rapidly than carbon dioxide, but when it's in clouds or a volcanic plume, it disperses more slowly, prolonging its potentially damaging effects.

Sam Carana, editor of the *Arctic News* blog, had been carefully observing the dramatically warmer north polar region. He explained that with the rise in temperature of the Arctic Ocean, more methane would be expected to escape from the sea floor and enter the atmosphere. This could then warm the atmosphere in that region and cause more methane eruptions to eventually warm the entire globe's atmosphere. A large enough burst of methane could reverse the carbon cycle, such that plants might release more carbon than they currently absorb. He explained that this is because the twenty-year global warming potential of methane is eighty-six times that of carbon dioxide, and such a sudden increase in methane could lead to a rapid rise in global temperature by 3°C or more, which could then reverse the carbon cycle.

Is this scenario of a giant methane "burp" from the Arctic sea floor just a scare story? Gregory Ryskin, the chemical engineer at Northwestern University referred to earlier, concluded that the Permian-Triassic (P-Tr) extinction (the "Great Dying") might have been caused by massive methane eruptions triggered by the overheated Earth and the disruption caused by mega volcanoes. Ninety-six percent of marine life and about seventy-six percent of terrestrial life went extinct.

According to Harold Wanless, professor of geology at Miami University in Florida, how this warming would develop remained unknown. Models show the trend of global warming, but they do not explain the rate that it might happen or what happens when there is a sudden shift. Methane can be released suddenly when the permafrost in Siberia and clathrates under the shallow waters of the continental shelves melt.

In a 2019 article in *News-Press.com*, David Trecker, a chemist and retired Pfizer executive, states that the National Oceanic and Atmospheric Administration's initial projection for the upper range of sea level rise by 2100 was 6.5 feet. More recently they increased that estimate to eight feet. Trecker also explains that Wanless said many scientists predicted up to 12.5 feet by 2100, with outliers as high as thirty feet; and that Robert Kopp, a climate scientist, geobiologist, and climate policy scholar at Rutgers said, "There are reasonably good estimates for how quickly the seas will rise until 2050. Beyond that the models become deeply uncertain." Wanless, who had been predicting ice melting rates and resulting sea level rises for years, suspected the situation could spin out of control quickly.

Professor Wanless may have hit the nail (and the naysayers) on the head. His assessment had been done before any of the IXonian aliens had shown up and unintentionally bombed a great many of the clathrate beds along the California shores and the littoral areas of Northern Alaska and Canada. Lesser amounts of methane were released along the East Coast of the United States and on the European continents, but the vast Siberian plains provided plenty of methane with the warming of the tundra's permafrost. Siberia didn't need any bombing to release its gases. Even though the methane volumes were already high, the volcanic eruptions in Iceland, and now in many other areas as the snow and ice covers were melting, added another level of heavy (often deadly) pollution to the atmosphere. Millions of birds were among the first to succumb to the badly polluted air.

So, there it was! Methane messing with life on Earth. As mentioned, Dr. Ryskin believed that the third major extinction that had occurred on Earth, the "Great Dying," was caused by vast methane eruptions in an already over-heated world 250 million years ago—hard to prove conclusively, but as Ryskin and the rest of the world watched and waited (breathlessly?), that third major extinction began to look like it might be getting repeated. Certainly neither Dr. Ryskin nor anyone else could have predicted that the world would be doing battle with methane-breathing aliens who were operating out of a base on

Jupiter's moon Ganymede, and who were possibly from a planet (IX) that no one was sure even existed.

Whatever the combination of events—war, global warming, aliens with a Frogdroid (Ranatron), methane eruptions, increased volcanic activity—the Earth continued to smother and wither for years. A few pockets in Mexico and South America escaped any serious methane-related damage (excluding Tierra del Fuego and some of its associated islands where battles had been fought with the alien scout fighters and where shorelines had been hit by the exchanges of bullets and bombs).

How long would a new extinction take? Ten years (as Dr. Wanless believed)? Ten centuries? Ten million years? And if a large-scale extinction were to occur, it's very likely there would be some survivors. Who would they be? The Desert-Dingo-Dingbat-Jihadists? Would there be some scientists and their offspring who could, over some centuries, gradually plan and develop how to truly control global warming, or continue the already started means of getting off Earth to find some habitable exoplanet or exomoon that the Earthlings could move to? It's so hard to predict. After the fifth extinction, when dinosaurs died out following their 160-million-year stint on Earth [i.e., the Cretaceous-Tertiary (K-T) extinction, also called the Cretaceous-Paleogene (K-Pg) extinction], how long did it take the small mammals that survived underground to evolve into *Homo sapiens* and other species?—Multimillions of years!

Mike and Molly McGowan lived long enough to see their grandchildren, but it was touch-and-go whether the grandchildren would survive the sparseness of fauna and flora, decreasing potable water, contaminated atmosphere, etc. that were menacing the world. Mike had developed a chronic asthmatic condition that limited his activity, but he and Molly did manage to survive into their eighties. They frequently reminisced about all they (and America) had been through.

Michael started with: "Of all the crazy things we could've ended up with. We had to contend with super-speedy flying robots, highly maneuverable rocket ships, and chasing a huge android that was part frog and part super-smart robot— Sheesh!"

Molly added: "I don't feel optimistic about the future—our species has done nothing but fight each other in the three to four million years since we climbed down from the trees and moved out of Africa. Now we have to take on some methane-breathing, methane-seeking aliens."

Michael began ticking off some of the many wars that had occurred in and around their lifetime. "Our grandparents were teenagers during WW I. Our parents were born just as WW II began, and they were in high school during the Korean War. We were born in the middle of the 'Cold War,' which lasted for forty-plus years and involved threats and counter threats with the Russians. They had been our allies during WW II, but turned to posturing about who had the most powerful weapons—atomic and otherwise. Add to those wars, the highly unpopular Vietnam War from 1955 to 1975, Desert Storm against Saddam Hussein and the Iraqis when they tried to invade Kuwait in 1990, Iraqi Freedom (called New Dawn in 2010) from 2003 to 2011, the elimination of Al Qaeda's Osama bin Laden in 2011, and ISIS/ISIL that continues to the present.

P.W. Singer seems to have been on the right track suggesting humankind (not just computers) is *Wired For War!*"

"There is so much fellowship, sharing, and support that could accompany so many religions and nations. Why couldn't that continue without the senseless jealousies, rivalries, fighting, and killing? Is it truly in our genetic make-up that competition and survival of the fittest make up the ruling law throughout all of the animal kingdom? Maybe we'll never be able to get peace and cooperation," Michael sadly contemplated.

Chapter 11

A fter the IXonians saw the massive amount of destruction that they had contributed to on the Blue Planet, they began to rethink their militaristic-investigative forays. They considered making peaceful contact with the Earthlings so they could combine efforts and join the Earthlings in investigating the massive universe beyond the solar system, the Kuiper belt, the Oort cloud, etc.

Maybe the IXon nation could even introduce their newly created Ranatrons to the Earthlings as helpful "beasts of burden." Perhaps this could help the Earthlings *frog*et about the past, join supercomputers with the IXonians, and head for outer space.

While the IXonians were working on new and better Ranatrons, their number one Rana had traveled back to Ganymede. The Ganymedeans left Rana #1 in a quiet recovery house where they could infuse his tired legs and figure out his next assignment. The atmosphere on Ganymede had a very small percentage of oxygen, and no methane. It is the only satellite in the solar system that has a magnetosphere (a region around a planetary body that shields that body from solar and cosmic particle radiation, making it potentially habitable), but the IXonians had to bring or manufacture their own life-sustaining methane.

Similar to NASA's ISRU (In-Situ Resource Utilization) practice of generating products with local materials during space travel, the IXonians had a process for generating methane using Ganymede's vast subterranean ocean as the substrate to initiate the Sabatier-like reaction. Electrolysis of water to create hydrogen gas (H_2, which can be used directly in fuel cells as well as in the making of methane), and the addition of CO_2 to create methane, would allow the production of this life-supporting gas instead of having to transport it all the way from IXon. For methane supplies brought from other locations, they also had methods to help eliminate some of the undesirable contaminants from the gases. For example, hydrogen sulfide and carbon dioxide can be extracted using amines such as diethanolamine (DEA) and monoethanolamine (MEA).

Before the smoldering Earth shut down almost entirely, there were enough operational aerospace sites (NASA and others) from where scientists could finally launch some of their long-researched nuclear-powered spacecraft—better than the low-thrust VASIMR's xenon-ionized propellant rockets—for quick flights within the solar system. David Neyland, head of DARPA (Defense Advanced Research Projects Agency), was one of the few rocket scientists who, along with NASA, preferred to continue developing the 100 Year Spaceship project. Seems like Neyland and Mae Jemison were both more interested in taking a hundred years to get a spaceship that could get humans far away from Planet Earth, rather than worrying about big frogs and little robotic geniuses from Ganymede and Planet IXon.

The aeronautical engineers at the NASA complex in Houston, Texas, a location that had fortunately avoided some of the heavy outpourings of methane from the West (California) and the North (the Arctic and the permafrost), had finally finished their elaborate tests on their nuclear-propelled rockets. The engineers began arranging to have some test pilots see if they could manage to control—and survive in—these superfast rockets.

Almost twenty-five years after the aliens and the Ranatron first visited Planet Earth, the Americans were ready to attempt a flight to Ganymede. Robert Link was the first to pass all the handling and survival tests required to operate the awe-inspiring, but still a bit nerve-wracking, nuclear-powered rocket. Link had the notion that the rocket should be named "Bobolink" after the migratory blackbird of North America. Of course he denied this had anything to do with his own moniker. The second pilot for this two-man spaceship was Gregory Nicols, who was dubbed "Dimes" for no apparent logical reason.

After a 398-day journey, Robert Link (who had adopted his rocket ship's name, "Bobolink," as his own), and Gregory "Dimes" Nicols arrived at a relatively flat surface between the ice and the rocky ridges that looked like sharp knives with the points directed upward. The retro-rockets were much more effective than any parachute could have been in the thin Ganymede atmosphere. The landing site was several miles from the IXon aerodrome, and the IXonians hadn't been alerted to any incoming flights. Nor were they expecting any visits from their faraway home on Planet IXon.

Another surprise for the IXonians around the aerodrome center was the whereabouts of Rana. A while after the scout rockets had returned, Rana was brought back to Ganymede and placed in protective custody to ensure nothing would happen to hurt their fantastic Frogdroid. His recovery hut was located about a mile from the aerodrome, and the IXonians expected that Rana might take a long time to rest and regain strength in his heavily used eight-foot-long legs.

Rana, however, was feeling a bit restless (and *Ranbunctious?*). Much sooner than expected, these legs that had been bio-engineered to leap tall buildings in a single bound, managed to force open the double-locked door of his protective shelter. When he gave a colossal kick, the door whipped open and he bounded away. Frolicking in the frozen countryside, Rana hopped and skipped away from his recovery hut—and away from the aerodrome.

Before any of the Ganymedeans were aware of Rana's escape, the great 'Tron spotted what appeared to be a couple of Earthlings. When he had gotten out of his rehab-house with now refreshed legs, he began following the instructions that he had received during his sojourn to the Blue Planet, where the Earthlings were recognized as "the enemy." His instructions were to either frighten or overcome Earthlings. Since this unexpected meeting with the Earthlings occurred about six miles away from the IXon base camp, Rana felt it was his duty to pursue these uninvited foreigners and not call for assistance.

Robert, the "Bobolink," and Gregory "Dimes" Nicols had not had any direct contact with the rambling, rumbling Rana, but with all the descriptions they heard from many of the military personnel back on Earth, they felt this was not a warm and fuzzy (slimy?) android with whom they would engage in any polite pleasantries. Both of the Americans had powerful jet backpacks—improved versions of the Mayman JB-9—that could give bursts of speed and elevation over limited time and distance. Powered by hydrogen peroxide with a silver catalyst, these jetpacks would come in handy if the operators had to avoid very rough terrain as they moved around Ganymede. The jetpacks would also come in handy if the Americans spotted the huge Frogatron bounding toward them—which they did!

"Time to be moseying along," Bobolink offered.

"Time for some change," Dimes Nicols agreed, as they both hit the start button and darted several hundred yards away from the big, bouncing bounder. They had to be very frugal with the firing of their jetpacks, realizing the fuel could be expended quite quickly.

It took a while for the IXon scientists to realize Ranatron had become a runaway (*Ranaway?*). It also took quite a bit of time for them to accurately locate him—might he possibly have ended up in one of Ganymede's frigid oceans?

The only true concerns the IXonian robotic engineers on this Jovian moon had were about replenishing 'Tron's legs and prehensile hands, and slowly building up his strength. His extremities were biological muscle, not mechanical, so like any extended muscular activity, it would take rest and time to allow for complete rejuvenation. The engineers' routine was to check on Rana every third day to be sure his supply of methane was still adequate.

None of the Ganymedeans had expected any foreign visitors—especially from Earth. After all, they knew its inhabitants hadn't developed any of the aero-technology that the IXonian scout rockets had. Consequently the Ganymedeans hadn't changed any of Rana's original orders or instructions.

They fully expected a quiet, peaceful recovery for Rana while they concentrated on working with some of the newer second-generation Frogdroids that they received from the mother planet far away in the Kuiper belt.

The scientific team on Ganymede never thought that Rana would break out of his quiet sanctuary and that the trotting 'Tron would be out and about chasing shadows or just gallivanting to loosen up his rehabbed legs and arms. They certainly didn't think he would be pursuing a couple of Earthling astronauts.

As Bobolink and Dimes used their jetpacks in short bursts to stay a comfortable distance ahead of the Ranatron, they had to carefully dodge around several deep holes in the icy surface of this moonscape. Rana, attempting to keep the two Jetsons in view, managed to take one of his giant leaps and unintentionally found himself at the bottom of a deep chasm. The Ganymedean gang that had gone looking for their fleeing Frogatron came within several thousand feet of the American spacecraft. They surrounded it and then waited for further instructions from their base camp. In the meantime, the galloping Ganymedeans had a chance to rescue their Rana-in-the-Ravine, but not without a snide remark from an IXonian: "You mean you couldn't jump out of this pitiful pit?"

The Ganymede base camp scientists needed to get in touch with the leaders back on Planet IXon to see how they should proceed with these strangers from a strange land. It would take many hours to get messages back and forth from IXon—which was well beyond Saturn—to the "jovial" Ganymede.

While time passed before the messages from IXon came through, the search team reached the traumatized 'Tron and returned him to his recovery house. This time they left a permanent guard so there would be no more Runaway Rana. After securing Rana, the Ganymedean guard surrounded the two American amigos and tried unsuccessfully to communicate with them. No one got anywhere with the squeaks, whistles, and sign language. Dimes tried to sing a few friendly verses from *Moon over Miami*, slightly altering the words to a French flavored: "Moon over mo(o)n ami" to see if the aliens could catch a non-belligerent tone or mood in this melodic exchange.

When it seemed clear to the brain trust on Planet IXon that these two visitors from the Blue Planet were not intending to do any harm, and that one of the astronauts tried communicating with a pleasant little tune, the leading scientists began work on using their super-petaFLOPS computers to analyze the Earthlings' speech (and songs). The Americans would point to objects and give their English definition or description starting with parts of their bodies, then objects around the Ganymedean environs. They even tried to produce signs and sounds of anger, friendship, happiness, hunger, fatigue, etc., which began to get translated. The interactions were probably not too different from when Columbus first met the natives on Guanahani island (later called San Salvador by Columbus) in 1492.

The nuclear-powered exploratory spacecraft from Earth, now sitting on one of the smoother sites on the otherwise rough terrain on Ganymede's surface, was running low on oxygen, and the astronauts were running low on food. It seemed like a long time before the Ganymede guards got the okay (after some lengthy debate among the IXon hierarchy) to engage with the astronauts and begin to formulate the primitive, but useful, translation that the IXonian robots could use with the Americans.

The availability of the vast underground ocean's salty water would be an enormous help in continuing the production of oxygen (and hydrogen) with the large electrolyzer unit that the Americans had. The Ganymedeans were using their version of the Sabatier method to produce their life-giving methane to feed their frogs and other marshland dwellers from the subsurface swamps of IXon. This also provided them with fuel for multiple uses.

It was fortuitous for the Americans to be met with a friendly reception by the Ganymede inhabitants, especially after they had been through such long angry battles on Earth. The IXonians had tried to protect their Ranatron while prospecting for methane deposits, and the Earthlings made like it was October 30, 1938 when Orson Wells' radio broadcast gave a vivid account of *The War of the Worlds* when the Martians were landing at Grovers Mill, New Jersey. The panic in 1938 was duplicated and intensified when the IXon scout rocket-planes began pelting many of the areas around the world—especially the oceans and shorelines—as they tried to frighten, and occasionally destroy, the Earth's defensive forces.

The large loads of hydroponic and frozen foods that helped sustain the US astronauts were augmented by Ganymedean food that could be decontaminated to eliminate most of the methane content. The Ganymedeans fed such sustenance to their frogs and other assorted amphibians, which were kept in large tanks that contained ocean water kept at a temperature similar to that of the underground lakes and swamps of their mother planet.

The robotic team that was running the Ganymede station really only needed some periodic adjustments and lubricants to keep all their mechanical and computer parts in working order.

If their stay was prolonged on Ganymede, there were replacement robots that could be brought in if any serious problems or mechanical failures occurred.

The American spaceship had been carefully scanned by an IXonian device that had the capability of penetrating not only steel, but also the carbon-nanotube shell. The scanning revealed only what appeared to be low-powered personal weapons that could be used for defensive purposes, not a threat to the still skeptical Ganymede guards who were puzzled by the size, content, and function of the radiation shield that protected the astronauts from dangerous exposure to the powerful rays from their atomic propulsion system.

The IXonians, despite their initial skepticism, seemed to have come to the conclusion that their own society, in that far distant planet way beyond Neptune, was quite a bit more advanced than the one on Earth. And since there were only two astronauts, the IXonians knew that they could easily defeat them if they did attempt any dangerous activity.

While the two Americans were working on translating "Gig-glub-clankswish," which they decided came close to "Welcome to Ganymede," the world back home was struggling. It had now been over twenty-five years since North Dakota experienced the first strange froggy day in Beulah Town, and began the "dread, dread, Rana goes bob-bob-bobbing along, along" (apologies to Ira Gershwin and Harry Woods). There was no "cheer up you sleepy head—get up, get out of bed—live, love, laugh and be happy!"—at least not for the next couple of decades. More likely: "A froggy day in Beulah Town—Had us low, had us down—We viewed the morning with alarm—The Dakota mountains had lost their charm!"

During those last twenty-five years, the global temperatures had continued to rise, as did the oceans. So many areas in the oceans were bubbling up with methane from their depths, and to an even greater degree from along the shorelines where the shallower methane clathrates had been disrupted and their gaseous contents emptied into the atmosphere during the Frog Invasion. This pollution continued to wreak havoc on all the vegetative life as well as animal and human life. And when mixed with some smoke, sulfuric acid, and ash from the proliferating volcanoes, the atmospheric potion was becoming quite deadly.

It was fortuitous for the Americans that the IXonian troops didn't get a good read on the extent of the damage to so many of the methane beds. Otherwise, the IXonians might have felt it wise to become more friendly with the two Earthlings, which could then spread to a friendship or collaboration with the rest of the Blue Planet, allowing the IXonians to tap into the purer methane than they had encountered in the Lakes of Titan and Enceladus or other moons of Saturn. However, such a friendship could have a positive result for the Americans, allowing both the Earth dwellers and the IXonians to share astronomical information that could help them investigate the problems and possibilities of exploring the universe.

Scientists from Earth had conducted significant amounts of developmental work on spaceships, propellants, exoplanets, etc. before the Earth began to succumb to excessive heat and a smothering atmosphere—some were referring to this atmospheric abomination as "Fire and Brimstone" or "Hell on Earth" and felt this was like the punishment that had rained down on Sodom and Gomorrah (Genesis 19:24). A few of the scientists were absolutely convinced it all started when former president Trump pooh-poohed the ideas that the world was in a serious global warming phase and that increases in coal burning and carbon dioxide emissions were contributing to this situation.

With the worsening conditions on Earth, and because of the disintegration of the working environment in so many aeronautical facilities around the world, the USA had aborted most programs on distant flights and exploration of the universe. Meanwhile, DARPA, as well as Mae Jemison, still had a lot of work to do on their 100 Year Starship project.

The "Daedalus" interstellar craft research group, who had incorporated their atomic fusion engine into the Bobolink fly-me-to-the-moon (Ganymede, that is) two-man spaceship, was working on something larger and more powerful. They were creating an improved protective devise to avoid radiation damage from outer space and from their own atomic fusion engine.

Research on electromagnetic and warp drives, which were still more science fiction than reality, had been curtailed. Maybe the super brainiacs on IXon could be helpful in furthering these proposed projects. The Earthlings did believe that the aliens had superior ultrafast and maneuverable scout rocket-powered planes. Thus, they contemplated the idea of befriending the guys from Ganymede, so they might be able to join forces and work together to continue, improve, and revise some of the USA's aborted programs for exploring the universe.

Back in Guadalajara, it was difficult to tell at times whether or not Michael McGowan's ramblings were part of the semiconscious state he had fallen into, with what looked like the final stages of his battle with asthma, bronchitis, pneumonia, and finally lung cancer. One of his last "ramblings" certainly could have had some scientific import. He murmured concerns about how the oceans were being flooded with fresh water from the melting glaciers. Would this influx of fresh water affect the thermohaline currents (like the Gulf Stream in the Atlantic)? Could the altering of these currents, over a long time, result in the beginning of a new ice age? Certainly some of the climatologists had felt this a possibility.

"Will we end up in a 'Snowball Earth' like we had a couple billion years ago?" With this frosty thought, Michael drifted in and out of consciousness. He hadn't heard any news of the IXonians and the Americans joining together or making plans to work together to explore the Milky Way . . . or beyond.

As Michael breathed his last few breaths, the world seemed to be doing the same—the sixth extinction had arrived. Eighty-plus percent of the Earth's species would not survive. Would the Earth come back as it had after the previous five major extinctions? Probably? Or would a new world begin with Planet IXon and Planet Earth combining efforts to begin an exploration of the universe? Would there be a new forceful species of giant Randroids that would become the soldiers of the IXon-Earth collaboration?

There were no clear answers even after a Giant Frog, Methane Smog, and Super Speed to Ganymede had changed a small portion of our solar system. Perhaps this extinction would cover up the definite denouement that was fast causing the sad decline and fall of America (and other nations?).

THE END? —THE BEGINNING?

Abbreviations and Acronyms

ACA	Affordable Care Act
AI	Artificial Intelligence
CE	Common Era
CH_4	methane
CO_2	carbon dioxide
COPD	chronic obstructive pulmonary disease
DARPA	Defense Advanced Research Projects Agency
DEA	diethanolamine
exaFLOPS	quintillion (10^{18}) floating point operations per second
H_2	hydrogen
ISIL	Islamic State of Iraq and the Levant
ISIS	Islamic State of Iraq and Syria
K-Pg	Cretaceous-Paleogene
K-T	Cretaceous-Tertiary
LNG	liquefied (synthetic) natural gas
MEA	monoethanolamine
MIT	Massachusetts Institute of Technology
NASA	National Aeronautics and Space Administration
NATO	North Atlantic Treaty Organization

NTREES   Nuclear Thermal Rocket Element Environmental
           Simulator
P-Tr   Permian-Triassic
petaFLOPS quadrillion (10^{15}) **fl**oating point **op**erations per
           second
psi   pounds per square inch
SNG   synthetic natural gas
UAV   unmanned aerial vehicle (drone)
UFO   unidentified flying object
USSR   Union of Soviet Socialist Republics
VASIMR   Variable Specific Impulse Magnetoplasma Rocket
VTOL   vertical takeoff and landing

Bibliography

Chapter 1

Kolbert, Elizabeth. *The Sixth Extinction: An Unnatural History,* First Edition. Henry Holt and Co., 2014.

Chapter 7

Colvile, Robert. *The Great Acceleration: How the World is Getting Faster, Faster.* Bloomsbury, 2016 (p. 321).

Chapter 8

Kelly, Kevin. *The Inevitable: Understanding the 12 Technological Forces That Will Shape Our Future.* Viking, 2016 (p. 291).

Chapter 9

Alden, Edward. *Failure to Adjust: How America Got Left Behind in the Global Economy*. Rowman & Littlefield Publishers, 2016.

Allison, Graham. *Destined For War: Can America and China Escape Thucydides's Trap?* Mariner Books, 2017.

Barfield, Woodrow. *Cyber-Humans: Our Future with Machines.* Copernicus, 2015 (p. 275).

Barrat, James. *Our Final Invention: Artificial Intelligence and the End of the Human Era.* Thomas Dunne Books, 2013 (p. 267).

Haass, Richard. *A World in Disarray: American Foreign Policy and the Crisis of the Old Order.* Penguin Press, 2017 (pp. 210-211).

Marshall, Bob, CPA. *A Sinking Nation—Unraveling the Complexities of the U.S. Debt and Deficit.* Dei Saphan LLC, 2016.

Newitz, Annalee. *Scatter, Adapt and Remember: How Humans Will Survive a Mass Extinction.* Anchor, 2013 (pp. 257-263).

Rachman, Gideon. *Easternization: Asia's Rise and America's Decline from Obama to Trump and Beyond.* Other Press, 2017.

Rickards, James. *The Road To Ruin: The Global Elites' Secret Plan for the Next Financial Crisis.* Portfolio, 2016.

Singer, P. W. *Wired for War: Robotics Revolution and Conflict in the 21st Century.* Penguin Books, 2009 (pp. 434, 436).

Chapter 10

Carana, Sam, editor. *Arctic News* blog.

Trecker, David. *News-Pres.com.* "Sea level rise is a problem for the future of Florida." April 23, 2019. *https://www.news-press.com/story/opinion/contributors/2019/04/23/sea-level-rise-problem-future-florida/3541452002/.*

About the Author

Dr. Robert K. Leet is a retired physician who loves to write science fiction and read almost anything he can get his hands on. With his Harvard University geology degree in hand, he worked on a scientific expedition in the Arctic Circle before embarking on his forty-year career as an internist. He began in aerospace medicine where he had the distinct honor of being kicked in the head by Neil Armstrong during a training exercise. Through his unique lens, he weaves together his experiences and interests in medicine, science, geography, and politics, providing a fascinating perspective to his writing.

He has three grown children, five grandchildren, and he lives in Shrewsbury, Massachusetts with his beloved wife of sixty-three years.